# Walking
## with the
# Hood

## C. S. Clifford

First published in Great Britain by Pen Press 2014.

This edition published 2016 by C. S. Clifford

ISBN: 9780993195730

Printed and bound in the UK

A catalogue record of this book is available from the British Library

Edited by Jo Clifford and Claire Spinks

Cover illustration and design by Claire Spinks

For all the children I have taught over the years, who remain a constant inspiration to me.

And to Jo, my wife, for her time, patience and love. Her formidable redrafting and language skills have helped hone this story to its final form.

Also by C. S .Clifford:

*Walking with Nessie* – ISBN 9780993195709 - 2015

**Coming soon:** *Walking with the Fishermen*

Find out more at **www.csclifford.co.uk**

To Bethany
Best Wishes
CSClifford

## Chapter 1

# The Waterfall

The two boys lay stretched out on their backs on the grassy bank of the river, listening to the sound of the waterfall cascading down the vertical cliff face towering above them. The midsummer sun was the only interruption to the flawless, azure sky and both had their eyes firmly shut against the glare of its radiance.

It was only the second day of the summer holidays, but they had been discussing the coming rugby season with enthusiasm. Neither was particularly gifted academically, but both had definite talent when it came to rugby and it was this that made long, boring schooldays bearable for them.

Dressed just in shorts, T-shirts discarded by their sides, they soaked up the heat with pleasure, their previous excited chatter silenced as they basked like lizards in the sun.

Their homes three miles distant, they had run most of the way here in a bid to begin the long journey to peak fitness by September when they would start playing their favourite sport once more. As money was difficult to come by at their age, and understanding the benefits of a good all-round exercise like swimming, they had decided to swim in the river as part of their training regime. The water here was only a few feet deep and not particularly fast-flowing, so on their limited budget it made a cheap alternative to the local swimming pool. Having decided on running and swimming, they had yet to include some form of weight training and the boys had discussed the possibility of using the woods to find fallen material to substitute for more formal gym equipment.

Matt, who had only recently had his fourteenth birthday, was one of the youngest in their year at school and was secretly quite proud of his recent muscular development, for he felt quite self-conscious about his shorter than average height. He had long, sandy-coloured hair that flapped carelessly across his face in the gentle breeze. His face had a rugged quality about it, with a broad forehead, strong jawline, and deep-set blue eyes. He was restless by nature, constantly in search of any sort of adventure to set his pulse racing, so much so that James often referred to him as his adrenaline-junkie mate!

In contrast, James, who would turn fifteen before half-term, was a head taller with a lithe body lacking the muscular tone of his best friend, but by no means less strong. His hair was shorter, dark and curly and his facial features softer, which perfectly disguised his determined nature and inner strength. While he too enjoyed feeling the rush of adrenaline in his body and appeared quite fearless, he did not actively seek out adventure the way that Matt did but was nonetheless happy to follow him on his madcap ventures. More than once this had led the boys into trouble at school, not for causing harm to others but for the potential of harm to themselves. They served their punishment without complaint, but within minutes,

Matt would reveal his next idea for adventure, which had James rolling his eyes skyward.

"Time for a swim, I think," said Matt, suddenly breaking the silence, his impatient nature exhausted with the apparent torture of ten minutes' inactivity. "Last one in's an idiot!"

Laughing, he rose quickly to his feet.

James had been waiting for this, knowing that his friend would not be able to lie still for much longer and was up the moment Matt started to speak. Like synchronised swimmers they dived into the water together, both heads appearing above the surface simultaneously. Serious training was forgotten as they splashed about, enjoying the coolness of the water after the heat of the sun, and launching waves at each other with their hands.

"Let's do some training," Matt suggested. "Ten lengths from here to the waterfall. It's about twenty metres there and back, that'll be two hundred metres flat-out sprinting."

"Only *ten* lengths?" asked James, a challenge in his voice.

"Ten for now and then some endurance stuff afterwards."

James laughed at that.

"You didn't think that was all I was planning, did you?" said Matt, grinning.

The boys set off quickly, knowing that the pace was too fast to keep up but not really caring. By the end of the laps, the pace had slowed considerably and the two of them panted exhaustedly.

"We need to get a lot fitter than this," said Matt,

disappointed with their performance.

"Plenty of time for that," replied James, hoping for a rest before the next challenge came. He climbed out of the water and sat on the grassy bank where Matt joined him.

"What we need is to build up our lung capacity; the more air we take in, the longer we can perform at top level. I think we should do some underwater swimming – that'll help improve it," he said.

"It's a good idea, but I think I'll rest for a while first. We're not going to improve much if we go at everything like a bull in a china shop," said James, philosophically. Matt nodded thoughtfully and lay back on the grass once more.

Within ten minutes, Matt announced that he was ready to try the underwater swim. James smiled at his friend's supposed patience and restraint. *A whole ten minutes, wow!* he thought, ruefully but obediently followed Matt into the water again.

"I've never really done much underwater swimming, so I don't know how far I can go. Let's do as you say and take it steady. Same course, from here to the waterfall and back, and see what we can do."

"Sounds good," replied James, pleased that his words had been heeded. "You go first!"

Matt set off, making it as far as the waterfall and half the distance back, before his head appeared above the water. James moved up to Matt's finishing position and ducked under. He swam strongly and surfaced back at where he had started from, secretly knowing that he could have gone much further.

They repeated the swim twice more before Matt

surfaced near the waterfall. He beckoned to James and waited while he swam over. James looked at him quizzically.

"There's something down there!" Matt told him excitedly. "I swam too far last time and the waterfall pushed me deeper. The bottom suddenly shelves down. I could see the cliff face and it looks like there's a hole in it – a cave. Let's go and explore!"

"How big is it? It has to be big or we might get stuck," said James, his interest piqued.

"It looks big enough. Take a look and see what you think."

James nodded, took a deep breath and dropped below the surface. For a moment, his feet surfaced as he swam down, then they too disappeared. It was a few seconds before he re-emerged.

"You're right! It is a cave, and it does look big enough for us to swim into. There's no way of knowing how far back it goes, so we'll need to be careful. I think it'd be better if we came back with an underwater torch and a length of rope or something."

"What do we need rope for?" asked Matt.

"It's dark down there. If it goes in a long way, we might get disorientated. We could tie the rope to something and take the other end with us; then we'd only have to follow it to get back out," James told him.

"I like your thinking, buddy; that makes sense. We'll come back tomorrow and do it. At worst, it won't go anywhere and just be a deep recess, but at best, who knows?" said Matt grinning, the adrenaline already flowing in anticipation. "Let's hang around for a bit longer though, it's too early to go back just yet."

The next day, the two boys returned to the same spot armed with a torch and a length of polypropylene rope. Matt didn't waste a second, securing it to an old tree stump a few metres from the waterfall. He unravelled the rest and tied the other end round his wrist.

"I'll go down first and check it out. Although the hole looks big enough for us both to get in, only one of us can go in at a time. If you follow too closely, I might not have room to turn round to come out."

"Sounds good," James told him. "But if I think you've been down there too long, I'll come in after you. I have your back covered!"

"I'll be fine! And when I get back, you can go," said Matt, the excitement building to a point where he just needed to get on with it. Typically of him, there was no sense of fear.

He started to take in deep breaths and release them until, without another word, he ducked below the water. James watched the rope disappearing, snaking off the riverbank where Matt had uncoiled it. He waited patiently, expecting his friend to surface any second, estimating he had been under for about half a minute. He counted another fifteen seconds. Still no Matt, nor was there movement on the rope...

Acting instinctively, he dived down into the water, reaching the hole. He could see the rope leading into the entrance and grabbed it as he entered. Immediately, all light disappeared and he entered a world of darkness. A sense of fear coursed fleetingly through him and he stopped swimming, pulling himself carefully along the rope.

The rope became taut and started to ascend, and he

extended his arm along it before moving upwards. His hand hit rock above him and he stopped, worrying that he would soon run out of air. He continued more slowly, following the rock almost vertically now until he saw light dancing above him. Suddenly, his head broke through the surface and he felt cool air on his face.

James took a deep breath and rubbed the water from his eyes. As they focussed, he could make out the silhouette of his friend standing up out of the water at one side of the pool, wielding the torchlight in all directions.

"You took your time, James – I thought I was going to have to come back and get you."

"For all I knew, you were stuck fast and drowning," James retorted.

"Some chance! Get yourself out of the water and come and see this," said Matt, the excitement in his voice as clear as daylight. James hauled his body out of the water and stood beside his friend.

"Watch the light!" Matt ordered and slowly began to move the beam around the cave. The light revealed a narrow tunnel, tall enough to walk along without bending. "Looks like we've got some exploring to do," he said with a gleam in his eye.

"Hold on a minute!" said James, stopping him before he could disappear down the tunnel.

"What for?" asked Matt, impatiently.

"We need something to mark our route, in case it goes on for a long way and branches off," James told him.

"Let's see if there's anything on the ground that will make a mark." Matt turned the torch towards the ground in front of them and immediately stooped to pick up a small, hand-sized piece of rock. He scraped it along the wall and nodded, "This should do it, it's almost as good as chalk."

Pleased with the result, he turned to James and grinning, asked, "So, are you ready for this?" and took the first step forward without waiting for an answer.

## Chapter 2

# The Tunnel

The tunnel twisted and turned deeper into the hillside and they walked for some time, James making arrow marks along the smooth walls, pointing in the reverse direction so that they led the way back to where they started from. As they rounded yet another bend, they could see a distant light source ahead and Matt switched off the torch.

"Do you see that light? It could be a way out!" he said excitedly. He switched the torch back on and continued forward. "I hear something up ahead!" he exclaimed. "What do you think it is?"

The roaring, rumbling noise sounded like distant thunder.

"I have no idea, but it's getting louder with every step," James responded, hoping that they might be able to get out soon; he was beginning to feel a bit claustrophobic.

Their pace increased in their excitement and as they rounded a final bend they were suddenly bathed in light, all but deafened by the roaring sound. They found themselves standing in a large cavern suffused in a strange but beautiful, greenish-blue light. Their eyes were drawn to the source of the loud noise.

"It's another waterfall!" shouted James, excitedly.

"We must have gone right through the hillside and out the other side," said Matt.

"We can't have done," shouted James above the noise of the water. "There is no waterfall on the other side. There are just sloping fields and a little stream. I used to go for walks round here with my parents when I was little, so I know the countryside like the back of my hand."

"You must be mistaken," Matt replied, but he too knew the area well and had never come across another waterfall. Despite this, there was undoubtedly another waterfall in front of them. "Maybe it's *our* waterfall; maybe we've gone round in a big circle and come back to it at a higher level."

James thought about it before answering.

"It's possible, I s'pose, but I'm pretty sure that this waterfall is wider than the one we swam under and there certainly appears to be a greater force of water falling here. I can't see through it here, yet we could see the cliff face through the water when we were on the other side."

"I think you're right," replied Matt, his eyes tracing the ledge from one side to the other. "There's a definite ledge here sticking out into the water. There wasn't a ledge on our waterfall; I think this one continues past the opening so it could be a way out of here. Shall we try?"

James felt a shiver of anticipation pass through his body.

"Let's do it! If we can't get out then we've found one cool place that nobody else knows about, and if we can, well, who knows what we'll find! We have plenty of time, so let's make the most of it."

"Absolutely!" said Matt, grinning like a Cheshire cat.

They peered out past the waterfall. The ledge reached

out about two feet and continued past the falling water. Matt stretched his foot out into the water to test the force of it, then inched it round the side of the entrance trying to feel how far the ledge went. His foot remained on solid ground.

"I'm going to try it. Hang on to my wrist, in case I slip," he yelled against the noise of the water. James nodded and locked his hand onto Matt's wrist.

Matt edged his way out and along while James watched his friend slowly disappear into the falling water. He felt Matt pull on his wrist and edged himself forward to allow him room to venture further. Then Matt gave him a couple of sharp pulls and he knew it was a signal for him to follow. He took a deep breath and stepped out into the full force of the water. As he edged along the ridge he felt the force lessen and the light intensity increase until, after another two small steps, he was out of the water. He wiped the water from his eyes and saw Matt further along the ledge.

"Can you believe this? Are you seeing what I'm seeing?" asked Matt.

James did not answer at first, focussing instead on the scene in front of him.

The ledge was about a metre off the ground. It petered out onto some large boulders which, in turn, led to the ground. The waterfall fell into a small pool which gurgled and glugged but with no stream or river running from it. James' first thought was that it must be draining underground and surfacing somewhere else. The ground beyond the pool sloped down and away from it. It was only when he looked at the area around it that he understood why his friend had expressed such incredulity.

The grass-covered ground around them led to an incredible mountain scene, with swathes of coniferous trees reaching up towards rocky peaks. It was a scene he had only ever witnessed in documentaries on television, pictures in books or on the internet.

"This cannot be real," he gasped in amazement. "We must be seeing things – hallucinating or something!"

Matt looked at him and laughed in relief.

"I thought that too, but now you're seeing it, I know that it's no trick of the imagination. Have you ever seen a place as amazing as this?" he asked, chuckling with delight.

"Never, that's for sure!" replied James. "This place is perfect for exploring."

"Let's do it then," said Matt, already caught up in the rush of excitement.

"Hang on a moment, we need to talk about this first. This place can't be real – it doesn't exist, at least not here. It doesn't even look like England—" James said but was interrupted before he could say any more.

"All the more reason for exploring it then!" interjected Matt.

"Good explorers do not go into the wilderness unprepared," said James, patiently. "Besides, if we got lost here, or hurt or something, nobody would ever find us. We haven't even got our mobiles with us. We need to go back and write a list of things to bring with us."

Matt looked disappointed but knew that his friend had raised a good point.

James edged back into the water, following the ledge into the cave before Matt could suggest anything else. He knew his friend had an impetuous nature, but he did not want to do anything risky, not without some sort of preparation.

Matt soon followed him inside, and they sat on the floor of the cavern making a mental list of things they would need: food, water, warm clothes, rope, penknives... They decided to come back the following morning, making an early start, and spend the whole day exploring the land they had discovered.

Before they left, Matt said he wanted to take one more look at this new land, so again they followed the ledge along its narrow, drenching path. Clearing the water from their eyes, they were shocked at what they saw.

"This can't be right! What's going on? What is this place?" asked Matt as they looked out at the scene before them.

"It's a tropical rainforest," stated James, far too matter-of-fact for Matt's liking.

"I can see that! But how can it be a mountain scene one minute and a tropical rainforest the next? We followed the same ledge out. There is no rainforest in Great Britain, except perhaps the Eden project in Cornwall."

"I have no idea what's going on, but I don't like it very much. We have to be dreaming or something – it's just too weird! I think we should go back," James said, already making his way back along the ledge.

Once in the cavern, Matt tried to delay James' plan to leave.

"We need to find out what's going on here before we go back. I mean, we've stumbled on something pretty unusual here, to say the least. If the land's changed once, then before we leave we need to find out if it'll change again, otherwise we'll be planning supplies for one place, only to find ourselves somewhere else."

"Ok, we'll go through one more time, but we are

*definitely* not exploring anywhere today. Alright?"

Matt nodded and led the way behind the waterfall once more.

They ventured out again, to be transfixed, awestruck by the astonishing sight of an arctic vista. In all directions, the landscape undulated gently, painted in hues of white, pale blue and soft grey. There was no visible sun, yet it was still light. There was no sound except that of a light wind gently whistling around their ears.

Despite the frozen scene, the waterfall kept flowing and disappeared into the pool beneath them. It was the only thing in their vision that was not frozen. Standing there in just a pair of shorts, both boys noticed that they were not feeling the cold as they should have been. James realised that he hadn't felt the heat and humidity of the jungle either.

Back in the concealed cave, they looked at each other, eyes aglow with excitement, breathing a single word as one.

"Wow!"

Matt picked up the torch and silently led the way through the long tunnel back to the pool. They lowered themselves into the water, took a few deep breaths and ducked under, following the rope back to their reality.

Chapter 3

# A New World

Clambering out of the river, the boys reached for their towels and dried themselves briskly.

"Well – that was different!" Matt exclaimed, pulling his T-shirt over his head.

"Not the sort of thing that happens to you every day."

"We need to scrutinise this before we forget any of the details. When did we first start to notice anything strange?" said Matt.

James was surprised by his friend's question. It was not like him to be so analytical. He didn't reply at first, concentrating on strapping his watch back on his wrist. He stayed quiet, staring at the watch before shaking it as if to check that it was still working.

"What do you make the time, Matt?" he asked.

Matt grabbed a small rucksack and pulled his watch from it. "Ten past two," he said, "Why? What d'you make it?"

"I make it the same, but that means..."

James' voice trailed off and he remained looking at his watch.

"Means what?" Matt asked, not quite understanding.

"Well, how long do you think we spent in the cave, in all I mean?"

"Well, let's see. We swam in, followed the tunnel, went through the waterfall, sat and discussed it, went back through twice more. I can't be sure, but I reckon about an hour and a half, maybe two hours. Why?"

"When I took my watch off before we went in, I noticed that it was two o'clock so unless both our watches have stopped, then our entire adventure has taken about ten minutes."

Matt didn't respond immediately as he considered James' revelation.

"Ok, I have an idea," he said, slowly. "Your watch recorded only ten minutes. That's about the time it took for us to get down to the cave and then back to the bank when we returned. Can you see where I'm going with this?"

James nodded a response before spelling it out.

"You think that time 'stood still' when we got inside the cave."

"When you think about what just happened, I don't see that it's any more unlikely than the rest of it," Matt continued.

"You know, it sounds almost plausible." He sighed heavily. "I don't really know what to think of all this."

"Ok, let's take it step by step. Did you notice anything strange on the swim down or as we went through the underwater cave?" Matt started.

"I didn't notice anything at all – you had the torch, remember? I swam by touch alone. What about you?"

"No!"

"What about the area with the pool?"

"It seemed to be a normal sort of cave. It had rubble on the floor. Wait! It had rough, uneven walls, not like the tunnel which had really smooth walls," continued James.

"I noticed that too. It was probably made by water, millions of years ago. What about the waterfall cavern – anything strange about that?"

"I didn't notice anything – it appeared to be a natural space. I've heard of caves behind waterfalls before, seen them in movies too."

"That just leaves what we found when we went along the ledge, then," Matt concluded.

"There's not much to say about that, except that it was a different setting each time we went out. But we didn't feel the drop in temperature. And why wasn't the waterfall frozen like everything else there?" asked James.

There was no answer to that, and they both sat quietly, lost in thought, desperately seeking plausible explanations.

After a while Matt stood up to stretch and wandered along the bank for a few paces before returning.

"You can laugh if you want, but this is what I think. The waterfall cave is a 'portal' to other places on Earth. Because time stood still while we were in there, I reckon we could explore without anybody knowing we were gone or worrying about us. We could stay as long as we liked, and then come back through when we've had enough. Imagine that – free travel around the world whenever we wanted!"

James nodded his agreement before adding his own thoughts.

"We just have one problem though, and that is that we can't choose our destination. Each time we go through, it's a different place. What if, when we try to come back, we also come back to a different place?"

"So far we have come back to our own place each time," Matt countered quickly.

"That's true. But we never actually stepped off the ledge, did we? So we can't guarantee this for sure. It could be that this portal acts the same in both directions, so we need to check this out before we explore anywhere."

"How do you propose to do that?" asked Matt, intrigued.

"What if one of us steps off while the other waits? We could tie ourselves together with rope or something."

"It's a good idea – let's go back and try it now!" Matt suggested.

"Hang on a sec! I think we should get some survival things together, so that if we do get stuck or lost, we're as prepared as we can be," said James, firmly, his tone indicating that there was to be no trip without preparation.

Undaunted, Matt's impetuous nature swung into gear immediately.

"Let's make a list then!"

James laughed at his impatience.

"No pencil or paper. We'll have to go home to do this. You can come round to my house – my parents are at work and we'll have the place to ourselves."

Matt was up and walking before James had even finished.

The next day could not come quickly enough for the boys, and both were up shortly after dawn. Neither had benefitted from a good night's sleep as their minds raced, filled with thoughts of adventure.

They met outside Matt's back gate, each carrying a backpack of things they thought they might need, and started the long walk to the river. With anticipation and excitement building, they approached the river and dropped their packs on the ground by the waterfall. The rope they had used the day before, was exactly how they had left it, snaking down into the waterfall.

Matt took out a wad of black, folded plastic bags and handed half of them to James. They put their rucksacks inside one, forced out as much air as they could and tied a knot at the opening. Then they sealed them inside two more bags, until the packs were tightly sealed and watertight. Then, with a look of readiness, Matt stood up and announced he was set to go.

James grinned.

"Let's do it!" He jumped into the water before Matt could even move, knowing how much it would irk his friend to have the lead position denied him.

They surfaced in the pool area and climbed out. Matt shone his torch around, examining each part of the space as if to check that it was still the same as it had been the previous day. Satisfied, he stood and led them along the tunnel to the waterfall cavern. Once there, he untied the bags encasing his pack, opened it up and drew out a length of thin but strong rope. He re-covered his pack before they tied the rope round each other's wrist.
Giving the thumbs-up signal, Matt made his way to the ledge with James right behind him.

They entered the water flow and edged their way along the ridge until they were free from the deluge. They looked out onto a densely wooded forest scene, the trees typical of English woodland. From the lavish greenery that enveloped the trees, it was clearly summertime, and dappled sunlight lanced its way to the forest floor creating an ethereal atmosphere.

The boys absorbed the view and nodded to each other, thinking that this looked like a suitable place to explore. Matt raised his tied wrist and edged towards the boulders so that he could climb down to the forest floor. James gripped the rope tightly, not really sure what to expect and watched his friend jump off the last rock and make touchdown. Both remained still as if waiting for something to happen, before Matt gestured for James to come down too.

They untied the rope from their wrists and took the plastic bags from their packs. James tucked them under a rock near the waterfall.

It was strange, looking at the waterfall from the other side. It looked natural enough and was fed from above by a large stream that raced down towards the rocky edge of a small hill. The unusual thing was that the water formed just a small pool in front of the cascade and seemed to disappear immediately underground.

Matt indicated with his hand that it was time to go, rather than shouting above the noise of the waterfall. After every five or six steps they looked back, as if waiting for something to change, but as nothing did, they started to walk with renewed confidence.

James had a stick of chalk ready in his hand and was periodically marking trees with arrows, pointing back to the waterfall, in case they lost their way.

After a few minutes, they came across a well-trodden path, narrow but easily visible, and decided to follow it. James marked the nearest tree with a very large arrow then decided to save the rest of the chalk for when they left the path.

They continued for about half an hour before a sudden noise halted them in their tracks.

"What was that?" Matt whispered.

"Haven't a clue!"

The sound came again.

"It sounds like an animal, a sort of grunt," said James.

"It's not like any animal I've heard before!"

Once again the noise came, then several at once followed by snapping sounds like branches being broken off.

"There's more than one of them," James whispered. "I think we should hide, just in case…"

The two of them edged towards a fallen tree lying at an angle on the forest floor. It was supported by one of its own branches, wedged against another tree. Ducking behind it, they waited, as the grunts grew louder and louder.

James risked raising his head above the trunk of the fallen tree. He could see patches of undergrowth moving vigorously ahead of them. Matt peered out too, his eyes following the direction indicated by James' finger. The noises became even louder with squeals alternating with grunts.

Then, with vibrations spreading through the ground before it, something large and dark came crashing out from the undergrowth, and they both ducked instinctively.

## Chapter 4

# John Little

Both boys stayed glued to the spot, unable to take their eyes off the scene unfolding in front of them.

"Pigs!" said Matt, laughing at the absurdity of the situation. "They don't look like ordinary pigs though, they're black and have weird tusks."

"I've seen pictures of these, they're wild boars, and can be quite ferocious and dangerous," James replied, uneasily. "We'd better stay here until they've gone."

"I'm not arguing, though I'd quite like to get a photo of them on my phone," replied Matt, his eyes still fixed on the animals.

"No, you'll make too much noise getting it out of your bag. We don't really want them to know we're here," whispered James.

The pigs moved slowly away, continuing their grunting and squealing until Matt decided he had had enough of waiting and stood up.

"Let's go!" he said, marching off without waiting for an answer.

They hadn't travelled more than a few hundred metres, when Matt suddenly stopped.

"What's that?" he asked.

James listened intently and could just make out the sound of whistling coming along the path towards them.

"It looks like we're not the only ones to know about this place. Somebody's coming!" he said.

As they rounded a bend in the track, they caught sight of a figure coming towards them.

The man raised his hand in acknowledgement and smiled as he noticed them. The boys returned the gesture, slowing as they approached him.

"Good day! Well, this is a surprise! If it is not Matthew Smith and James Thatcher. I have not seen ye these six or seven years! 'Tis good to see ye once more.

"I can see by the looks on your faces that ye do not recollect me. 'Tis William, William Cooper from Abbottsbury. There can only be two reasons for ye to be this far in the woods, and that is to seek the sanctuary of the Hood or to pledge allegiance to him. Either is a good choice lads, ye will not regret it. I, myself, am on a task for him at the moment so, alas, I cannot pass time with ye. I must away. If ye follow the path a while longer, ye will find the place ye seek. Good day to ye!"

"You too!" responded James, while Matt just nodded, dumbstruck. They watched him disappear round the bend in the trail.

"Oh my God – how weird was that?

"He knew us! He called us Matthew Smith and James Thatcher, but I've never seen him before in my life! We'd have been just little kids six or seven years ago – how could he remember us?" said James.

"Is he for real? Did you notice the clothes he was wearing? They were completely old-fashioned," observed Matt.

"Well at least he got our first names right," Matt laughed. "He talked like he hadn't spoken to anybody in years, scarcely taking a breath. He spoke funny too."

"It was lucky we didn't have any awkward questions to answer. How can he possibly recognise us though? We don't come from around here; we've never even been here before. He didn't talk to us like we were kids, either. This is definitely weird!" stated James, scratching his head.

"He reckons we're here to join the Hood, whatever or whoever that is, and that it's not far from here. I say we check it out – what do you think?"

"Well, we might get some answers that way. Yeah, I'm up for it," James replied.

"Another photo opportunity lost!" said Matt giving his customary grin that signalled his excitement at something new, and started down the path once more.


They were now much more attuned to the environment in which they found themselves. They were noticing more, hearing more; in fact, their senses seemed much more acute as they passed through sporadic shafts of misty light that reached towards the forest floor.

Stopping again as they heard rumblings through the trees, they marvelled at the sight of a small herd of red deer crossing the path, that seemed completely unconcerned about the two boys' presence.

It truly was a beautiful forest. Many of the trees were ancient oaks with stout, sturdy trunks soaring into the sky above, though there were many others, most of which they recognised. They could hear rustling above them, evidence of a wisp of wind, but they could not feel it at ground level, such was the protection that the trees offered. They heard a variety of birds chirping and tweeting above them, and the boys walked in silence for some distance, absorbing the richness of their surroundings.

They stopped to eat the sandwiches and apples they'd packed earlier and then continued along the path. It wasn't long before they picked up the sound of trickling water somewhere in the distance. James hoped that the trail led towards it, so they would not have to leave the path to find it. The route, so far, had been straightforward and easy to follow, should they need to retrace their footsteps in a hurry, and he didn't want to lose the security offered by the trail.

Ahead they could make out a much lighter area, perhaps the indication of a clearing. The path stopped abruptly at its edge and the sound of running water grew louder. Tumbling from the rocky outgrowths from the swell of the hillside, a wide channel of water cut a shallow course from one end of the forest clearing to the other, broken by a succession of tiny rapids, before narrowing abruptly and disappearing as a fast-flowing stream between rocks into the forest. They could see that, in places, the water was less than knee-high, but deeper pools were also indicated by areas of dark, still water.

"Well, that's the end of the trail. We could follow the water course upstream or cross it to see if the path continues on the other side of the clearing," suggested Matt. "What do you think?"

"Let's cross and see if the path continues," replied James, who wanted to be certain of finding their way back easily.

Matt grunted his agreement and stepped forward, taking the lead. The ground here changed radically, from the firm but dusty path to that of a shingle beach. The unevenness demanded their concentration as they started to find larger rocks to use as stepping stones to cross the shallower sections of water. They were about halfway across when they noticed a huge figure of a man standing directly in their path just ten metres ahead.

Matt saw him first and stopped abruptly. James, close behind, walked straight into him and would have lost his balance had Matt not grabbed his arm to steady him. James was about to say something in annoyance when he too caught sight of the figure.

"Who goes there, then?" the voice boomed across to them, the volume matching the size of the man himself.

Matt and James remained where they were and said nothing.

"Have ye no tongues in your heads? Who are ye and what business brings ye here?"

"Matthew Smith and James Thatcher at your service! We're here to see the Hood," answered Matt, more confidently than he really felt.

"And why would Robert of Loxley want to meet the likes of ye?"

James was beginning to feel irritated by the way they were being spoken to and tried to change the subject.

"Where we come from, it's customary to exchange names when you meet someone for the first time."

"It may be your custom, but here we have customs of our own!"

"Who is 'we'?" asked Matt.

"The people of the forest, of course!" the huge man returned. "And pray, where exactly do ye hail from?"

"South of the forest. We've been travelling a long time

to get here," James told him, still annoyed by the man's attitude towards them.

Matt and James became aware of other figures appearing silently from the forest around them, until they were completely surrounded.

"Well lads, ye need to know the way of things in these parts; to cross the river ye shall have to pay a charge – call it a tax if ye please."

"A tax? It sounds like extortion. What is this so-called *tax* for?"

"That is no concern of yours. But if ye pay, we will let ye pass."

"I am afraid that we are not carrying money or anything else of value," answered Matt, honestly.

"I was hoping ye would say that! If ye have no money, ye shall have to fight me for the right to cross."

"Look, I've had enough now. We're not part of your re-enactment group. Find someone else to play with – we just want to pass by."

"Ye are mistaken, lad. This is no act!"

The boys turned to each other in disbelief. "We can't fight him, Matt – look at him, he's huge! We could get badly hurt. I wonder what the mobile signal's like here. Perhaps we should phone my dad?"

"Don't be daft, James, how would anyone find us at all? Let alone in the next two minutes! We have no alternative. I think we might be able to surprise him with a thing or two, though!"

James looked at him as if he was losing his mind.

"What could we do to surprise him? He's bigger even than any rugby player I've ever seen."

"That's true, but I have a feeling that rugby is not a

game he knows much about!"

"It doesn't even seem to have been invented, yet!" said James, gloomily. "What's your idea then?"

"Charge him and tackle him rugby-style but at waist level. If we hit him hard enough we might just wind him, and while he's not at full strength, we could pin down his arms and legs."

"What about the others? I can't see them standing by and watching us get the better of him without getting involved."

"James, sometimes you worry too much! Look at him – how do you think he'll feel if the only way to beat us is with help from his friends? Ego, James, ego! I'll taunt him with it if the others threaten us. I can't see any other option."

The boys turned back to face the giant.

"We just want to pass by peaceably. There's absolutely no point in fighting, just to cross a river," James called out to him.

Matt didn't wait for a reply and confidently started to move towards the figure blocking their way. James moved to his side.

"When I call it, charge him and hit him with all your strength," Matt told him in a low voice.

They moved within four paces of the giant when Matt said, "Now!"

The speed at which the two of them moved surprised the big man and before he could adjust his position, the two of them crashed into him, each burying a shoulder into the man's waist. They achieved the result that Matt had been hoping for. The man went backwards and lost his footing, falling almost in slow motion, and grunting as the wind was forced out of his lungs.

The boys landed on top of him and quickly pinned down his arms. The giant thrashed his legs about in frustration, but they were safely out of reach of the boys. Matt noticed the others moving forward towards them and played his last card.

"Oh here we go! Going to allow your friends to help you out of this sorry situation, are you?" he said, using his best sarcastic tone.

The giant snapped out an order and the approaching men stopped abruptly.

"Perhaps you'll let us pass, now?" James asked.

"Yea, yea – ye can pass. Just let me up,"

Matt looked at the circle of men surrounding them and shouted, "You heard him! He said we can pass."

A gap appeared in the circle, in the direction that they wanted to go, and Matt slowly released the pressure he had been applying to the man. James followed suit and they both stood up. Matt offered his hand to the giant who took it and stood up in front of them.

"Ye boys hit hard," he said in grudging admiration. "I am a man of honour. Ye are free to pass. But not before I have a little retribution…"

Before James and Matt could register what he said, they found themselves flying backwards through the air as they were launched, with some force, into one of the deeper pools. They sank below the surface and reappeared coughing and spluttering from their unexpected immersion, to the sound of laughter from the men.

"Oh blimey!" said Matt to James, treading water. "What about our mobiles?"

The giant, still with a grin on his face, extended his

hand to Matt, who took it gratefully. But instead of using it to haul himself from the pool, Matt braced his feet on a submerged rock and pulled with all his might, so that the giant landed in the water beside them with a loud splash.

The circle of men laughed all the more and Matt and James joined in. The giant looked about him, momentarily nonplussed, before his face softened and he laughed with them.

Chapter 5

# The Clearing

The onlookers moved towards the edge of the pool, and several hands reached out to help them from the water. As the boys wiped the water from their faces, the talking and laughter suddenly stopped as a newcomer made her way through the group of men.

An angry voice broke the sudden silence.

"John Little! How many times have I told thee not to go using your might against people smaller than thyself? Thou great oaf!"

The giant had the decency to look abashed, before declaring that there were two of them! Someone called out that he had more than met his match and the laughter returned.

Matt and James looked up to see one of the most beautiful faces they had ever seen, smiling down on them. The smile radiated with such force that both were instantly captivated by her beauty.

Long, blonde hair tied back neatly in a ponytail reaching down to the small of her back, fluttered gently in the breeze. Startling, green eyes gleamed down at them in amusement at their sodden state.

The young woman was dressed in different shades of green; tight trousers accentuated her long legs while an olive green tunic buttoned tightly from top to bottom highlighted the startling white collar and cuffs of the blouse she wore beneath.

"Where do ye hail from? What business have ye in Sherwood Forest?" she enquired.

Matt looked quickly at James, a sudden realisation hitting his mind. James caught the look and gave Matt an almost imperceptible nod as the same thought occurred to him.

"These are questions we have already answered, but as yet, we have received no such courtesy from those challenging us," said Matt, politely.

John Little, somewhat provoked by the rebuke he had received from the woman, interrupted. "Their names be Matthew Smith and James Thatcher. They have travelled from south of the forest, Maid Marion; and verily, I have not had opportunity to introduce myself."

"Do not make such excuses with me, John Little. I know full well how thou reacts to strangers, and how much thou needs the indulgence of displaying your physical prowess," the young woman told him.

John faked a look of great hurt as he looked up at her, but James did not miss the affection in her eyes as she held John's stare, until he had the sense to look away.

"I am Lady Marion, first cousin to King Richard, and this oaf here is John Little. I am pleased to make your acquaintance. Anyone capable of giving this big bully a bath is most welcome in this part of the forest!" she said, again bestowing her radiant smile on both of them.

There was still a little laughter permeating the group of onlookers, but it ceased immediately when she glanced directly at the culprits.

"Good to meet you, Lady Marion," started James. "I think your arrival was just in time to prevent a rematch with Little John. I would hate to have to embarrass him for a second time," he said with a smile, looking in John's direction. He saw the big man raise an eyebrow at the tease but smile nonetheless.

"Thou hast spirit, James Thatcher, I'll give thee that. But think twice before challenging this man, for he is the largest in these parts. What brings ye both to Sherwood and how is it that ye both speak with a strange affliction to some of thy words? The people from the south I have met before do not share this difficulty."

"We have come to join the Hood. A friend of ours, William Cooper, told us how to get here and said we would be welcome," Matt exaggerated.

"We have travelled a lot in the past few years and I suppose the different dialects we have experienced have slipped into the way we talk," James added hastily, trying to cover up the obvious differences in how they spoke.

"Welcome to ye both. Robert needs all the men he can rally, especially a blacksmith like thyself. There is work also for a thatcher. Why don't ye follow us back to our village and see how hospitable the people of the forest can be."

"Thank you, Lady Marion, we would be happy to," replied Matt.

Marion and John Little led the way, with Matt and James close behind and rest of the group following.

"You thinking what I'm thinking?" asked Matt in a low voice.

"What, about it being a re-enactment? Yes, it must be – but their costumes are really good!"

"Idiot! No, do you think it's possible that we have actually gone back in time?"

"Well, I always thought that Robin Hood was just a legend. If he lived at all, it was hundreds of years ago in the time of Richard the Lionheart and all that. If we are here, it means that not only did we enter a new world through the waterfall but in a different time period as well," James told him.

"I suppose it does explain why we thought that William was dressed so differently. They're all dressed like this."

"What I find strange is that they haven't commented on how *we're* dressed differently, and they don't even seem to see us as boys. John Little wouldn't have challenged boys like that surely? After all, it wouldn't have improved his street cred one bit," reasoned James. "They speak differently from us, too."

"I noticed something else too. You might think this is a bit weird, but heck, everything that's happening is weird! I saw a film about Robin Hood once with Kevin Costner playing the part of Robin. On his way through Sherwood, he was met by John Little and challenged to a fight after he refused to pay a passing fee, just like us. The fight was different because they had sticks, but it happened just like it happened to us, even down to John Little being pulled into the pool. It seems too similar to be coincidental," Matt told him.

"I've seen that film too and I know what you mean. It's as if our past experiences are being used in the adventure we're having – but that's impossible, isn't it? I'll tell you what though, I'm quite enjoying all this and if time is standing still in our world, then we are going to experience one long summer holiday this year, especially if we go to other places and have more adventures," James concluded.

"You're right, I'm enjoying this too. Let's just go along with this and see where it takes us," replied Matt, grinning at the prospect. "But we'd better keep our phones and watches out of sight!"

They walked for a couple of miles further, before their ears caught the clatter of metallic clinks and hammerings along with mellower sounds of the forest. As the noise intensified, Matt suggested it sounded very much like sword fighting. James nodded his agreement just as John and Marion stopped in front of them.

"Watch your footing as we descend, it can be slippery at times. If ye lose your footing here, there's nothing to stop ye before the bottom," Marion cautioned.

At first the boys did not understand the warning, but then Marion and John seemed to disappear into the ground as they crossed over the edge of a large precipice and started down a rough path that bordered an almost vertical drop into a massive clearing below. The boys stared in amazement at the view. At the bottom of the clearing several dwellings had been constructed from the trees of the forest, while many more had been built into the trees themselves.

A stream crossed the clearing, supplying all the fresh water that the camp needed, and several fires burned brightly with a number of cooking pots giving off a variety of delicious food smells.

"Wow – this is some place, James! Just look at it!" Matt gazed around in awe and with a growing appetite for some of the food they could smell.

There was little light, apart from the shafts of sunlight reaching the forest floor, but there seemed to be a sort of green mist pervading the camp which added to the dreamlike quality of the setting. A large number of people below were each busy with their own tasks, creating a hive of industry. There were men working together erecting new buildings, each in a different state of construction; women attending to cooking and washing chores. Some women had even joined the men in practising sword-fighting, or with bows and arrows, aiming at targets set into the trees out of harm's way. Matt could even make out a blacksmith hammering away at a length of red-hot metal. This was more than just a camp; it was a large village concealed in the depths of the forest.

As they descended the track, they approached the height of the houses built into the trees. They could see how they had been constructed and how they were attached to the trees themselves. Each building had a simple ladder at each side of the structure, leading easily to the forest floor. Children sitting in small groups waved at the travellers as they passed by, giggling and hiding shyly when their greetings were returned.

Reaching the bottom, John stopped, while Marion continued along the well-trodden path. "Ye will do me the honour, I hope, of visiting with me and meeting my family. Ye must have a great hunger, as do I! What say ye?" he asked them.

"You're right there, John, I could eat a horse!" said Matt, appreciating the offer.

"Me too!" added James.

"Follow me, then. We have no horse meat, but ye can try some of the Sheriff's venison and my wife's fresh bread. We can share a jug of ale too, for I have such a thirst."

Before they had gone another five paces, his huge voice called out.

"Come hither, Mistress Heather, we have guests. Bring out more bowls and bread to go with that lovely stew of thine."

From behind a wooden structure appeared the biggest woman James had ever seen.

"Thou canst take care of that, thou stupid, unthinking, dolt. If I have told thee once, I have told thee a hundred times to give me warning when thou bringest somebody to eat with us."

"Don't mind her, lads – her bark is worse than her bite!"

"I heard that, John Little! Wouldst thou like to put that to the test?" she asked, coming at him armed with a huge wooden ladle. She swung it just once and the unfortunate John was too slow to get out of the way. It caught him high on the arm with a loud thwack.

Matt and James could not stop themselves from grinning, but their smiles quickly disappeared as she turned towards them.

"Wilt thou not introduce thy guests like a decent human being, or shall I do it myself?" she asked John, haughtily.

"Now then, good wife, do not take on in this way! Come hither and give me a big kiss."

Before she had time to respond, he had embraced her in a bear hug and covered her cheeks with kisses.

"Get off me, thou great oaf," she said, trying to break free. Her cheeks reddened with embarrassment, but at the same time, she was obviously enjoying the show of affection from her husband. John set her free and introduced the two boys, saying that he had met them at the river, without giving details of the incident there.

John's wife smiled warmly at them and invited them to sit down, while she went to finish preparing the food.

Returning a few minutes later, she served them each a large bowl of venison stew with a hunk of fresh bread about the size of a small loaf in most supermarkets.

'No wonder John is so huge!' Matt found himself thinking. He was glad that the silence of eating spared them from having to answer awkward questions.

When they had finished, John poured them each a tankard of ale from a large barrel that lay next to the dwelling. The boys drank it thirstily, not quite knowing what to expect, and were surprised at its fairly mild flavour.

"Made by these very hands," John told them, examining his overly large fingers. "Nectar of the Gods, but it will give ye a foul head if ye drinks too much of it."

Both knew instantly they would not be able to drink it in any sort of quantity.

"Not sure if I have too much room left for this, not after that fantastic stew," Matt said, honestly.

"Your wife is a good cook!" said James, and John beamed at the praise for his wife's domestic skills.

"We shall rest awhile and then I will show ye around the settlement. Robert will not be back for many hours, so ye can meet him this eventide. Just lie ye back and enjoy the fruits of free men," he told them, pouring more ale.

Chapter 6

# Robert of Loxley

Two hours passed, before the boys awoke simultaneously. Matt grinned at James.

"All this healthy lifestyle is catching up with us, I reckon. I never fall asleep in the day!"

"I think it's more likely to be the beer we had with lunch," replied his friend, massaging his temples. "Have you got a headache too?"

John heard them talking.

"Ye have awoken at last! Let us wash at the stream, then I will show ye the lay of the land."

Both boys felt more refreshed after rinsing their hands and faces in the stream. They drank some of the cold, clear water and began to show more interest in the scene around them.

"How long have you lived here?" asked James.

"Me and my goodly wife started the camp two years ago when I became a wanted man. The only place to go when ye have a price on your head is Sherwood Forest. There are many superstitions told of this place; some say 'tis haunted and some believe that it hides witches and other magical and mysterious creatures. Many think that it be cursed! But I never believed in such things and came right to the very middle with a few trusted friends to start this small community. Just about every man here is wanted for something, mostly for not having enough money for the outrageous taxes the Sheriff demands of us. He took every penny we had and still wanted more. Some of our women even have prices on their heads!

"Here though, we feel safe, and the forest supplies us with just about everything we need. Over the months, more and more people have taken refuge in the forest with us, and then one day, Robert of Loxley joined our group. The Sheriff had killed his father and seized his land, so when he returned from the crusades he had nothing left to come back to. We chanced upon him in the forest one day, and since then, he has become our leader. He is a good and fair man who knows how to get things done. One day he will marry Maid Marion, but he has sworn to get his lands back before that can happen. She is a fine woman too, brave and good, not a bad bone in her body." He stopped for breath and to introduce the first group of inhabitants they approached.

"These are some of our fighting men. Robert taught them how to use the sword and knife, to fight like knights and they practise their skills hither every day. I consider that ye two would do all right in this area, but ye also have other skills that we need elsewhere."

Approaching the next group, they saw that each man held a long bow and was firing arrows at a target about fifty metres away.

"Ever let loose an arrow from one of these?" asked John.

"No, but I'm willing to try," said Matt, eagerly.

"Well, that is easy to remedy. Michael, bring me a bow and some arrows!" he called out to a dark-haired man.

Michael brought the weapon to them.

"More recruits to join the fight, John?" he asked, hopefully.

"Perchance, but they have other skills. Let us see how they fare, shall we?" replied John.

He loaded a bow, took aim and watched with satisfaction as it hit the straw target in the distance. He handed the bow to Matt who followed his example. The arrow missed the target only by a few inches and John grunted in pleasure and congratulated him.

"Thank you!" said Matt, enjoying the praise although disappointed that he had missed.

"Remember to look along the length of the arrow using just one eye, until thou findest the target, then release the bowstring as gently as thou wouldst stroke a baby bird…"

Matt passed the bow to James, who took it, loaded an arrow, took careful aim and let it fly. It hit the target with a resounding thump.

"'Tis not easy for a beginner at this distance," said John. "That was most valiant for a first attempt!"

"I just followed your good advice," James told him, delighted with his success.

They left Michael and his men to continue their practice, and walked toward the sound of a hammer hitting metal.

"This is our smithy and where we make our weapons. Andrew!" he called. "Come and meet one of your own!"

A short, stocky figure with large, well-developed forearms ceased his hammering and came towards them.

"Well, this be a surprise – Matthew Smith! I have not seen thee for many a year, how fare thee?" he asked, extending his hand for Matt to shake.

"You know him?" John asked in disbelief.

"More than know him – I learnt my trade with his father. Even as a young boy this lad showed the promise of becoming the finest blacksmith in the land—"

Matt interrupted, "Good to see you again, Andrew. I'm pleased to see that my father's training has not gone to waste!" he said, immediately playing along with the role that had befallen him, and nodding at the craftsmanship of the newly forged swords standing in a row where Andrew had been working.

"Thou shalt be joining me then, I hope?" Andrew asked, warmly.

Matt nodded, "Unless the Hood has other plans for me. I just hope I'm up to the mark!"

They spent another hour being shown around the woodland village, stopping and talking with a variety of people who seemed very content living in this unorthodox community. They met a group of carpenters swarming over a newly constructed building and told them that James would be joining in with the thatching of the new structure.

The final dwelling they came to was occupied by a large group of children of different ages. John told them that it was a school, the first one of its kind built for peasant children. It was the specific project of Lady Marion's as she was the only one, apart from Robert, who could read and write. It was her intention that all the children of the forest should learn these skills and learn the French language as well. James could just make out Marion's blonde locks at the centre of the boisterous group of children.

"'Tis time to return," John announced, suddenly. "Robert will be back anon and I am anxious to introduce ye both to him. Newcomers have become much fewer these past seasons, so 'tis a rare occasion having ye arrive today. T 'will not be long before ye see why so many of us would lay down our lives for this man."

Matt exchanged a look of horror with James at the mere suggestion of doing anything as dramatic as that but refrained from commenting. Instead, he smiled and followed the big man back to where they had begun their journey.

The light was fading fast now and shafts of sunlight no longer penetrated right down to the forest floor. Instead, as the sun became lower on the horizon, it sent its rays horizontally through the canopy creating an almost misty, ghostly effect above their heads. Torches of plant material soaked in oily fats started to appear by the sides of the different homes and along inter-connecting pathways, spreading a warm, welcoming glow. Away from their direct light, people moved around as silhouettes in the increasing gloom; animals too, added to this shadow puppet scene amongst the trees.

John led the two boys back to his home and introduced them to his five children, the eldest three of whom seemed intent on play-fighting with him as soon as he appeared. He took the pounding good-naturedly before announcing that they would eat at the big clearing as soon as Robert returned. This, he explained to the boys, was a communal gathering area where meetings and feasts were regularly held, for the smallest of reasons, but which had become very important to the people of the forest in helping them become a tight-knit community.

Apparently, Robert was going to speak after they had

eaten, about a forthcoming venture that was big enough to involve all of them, and deal with any outstanding community issues. The boys were looking forward to this, keen to see how the community ran itself, to say nothing about the excitement of meeting the legendary Robin Hood himself!

Matt asked John how it was that Robert had become Robin and was told that it had happened for different reasons.

"The people here know him as Robin of the Hood; few are told of his true title, in case of capture and torture. His true identity is still unknown to the Sheriff and his men, although he has been hunted by them for many months now. The name Robin was chosen, at first, because somebody said that in a fight he was so quick, agile and brave that he was like a robin stealing crumbs from a table.

"Then there is his favourite pastime – his habit of robbing from the rich and giving to the poor, and is a play on the word 'robbing'."

Robin's surname, 'The Hood,' had been given to him by Will Scarlett, one of Robin's closest friends and was intended to give Robin a name that instilled fear amongst his enemies.

"'The Hood' sounds mysterious and fearsome," explained the giant man. "An unknown warrior from whom nobody is safe ... Except us in the forest, of course!

"And so Robert of Loxley became Robin Hood, friend of the poor and enemy of the rich. Speaking of Robin, 'tis time we gathered in the meeting area. There are such a number of people hither that seating can oft be a problem. 'Tis better to go afore time."

He called to Heather who arrived carrying a large pot of the same stew that they had devoured earlier. Behind her trailed John's children carrying a multitude of loaves, bowls and spoons. John's eldest son carried a flagon of mead. He was only twelve but was already showing signs of growing as tall as his father. John led the way, while James made himself popular with Heather by offering to carry the stew. She accepted his offer and made a mental note to speak to her husband about his own lack of manners.

The communal area was vast, and people were already sitting in their favourite spots. Without tables or chairs, people sat on matting or animal skins on the ground. John indicated the huge trunk of a fallen tree and told Matt and James that this was where Robert and Marion would sit so that they could easily see and be seen by those who wanted to speak. He told them that no comment was too small for Robert to listen and respond to, and anybody was free to speak. It was only when everyone had finished that Robert would speak about other matters and relate plans for any forthcoming venture he had planned.

"'Tis the only place in England where all men are treated as equals, no matter whence they came, and have the right to speak their minds. The people here respect Robert most of all for that."

Heather laid a large rug in their favoured place close to the fallen tree, and the children helped to arrange the food and bowls upon them. Even as they watched, the area was filling rapidly with other forest dwellers. Many tipped their hats to John and Heather as they passed them; some acknowledging his two guests too.

Matt and James were filled with excitement and anticipation of Robin Hood's imminent arrival.

Not five minutes had passed before the enigmatic

figure himself strode through the crowded gathering, stopping to greet many of the individuals seated there. He was accompanied by Marion who looked breathtakingly beautiful, attired as she was in a floor-length, emerald-green dress. James noticed how the men coloured slightly as she, like Robin, paused to talk to some of the people, many becoming tongue-tied when faced with her beauty and kind words.

By contrast, the men who had the opportunity to talk to the tall, athletically built Robin, sat taller themselves – proud at being selected by their champion for conversation. Robin shook hands with those he could not talk to, trying to welcome as many to the gathering as he could. He took an age to reach his seating place, and the minute they sat down, Heather took each of them a bowl of her stew and a clay goblet of mead.

"This was *borrowed* from the Sheriff's own storeroom!" she whispered, conspiratorially, as they sniffed at the sweet-smelling liquid.

Before he ate a single mouthful, Robin Hood raised his own goblet and shouted, "To the people of Sherwood Forest!" his voice carrying easily across the clearing, and to which everybody responded with the same toast.

Matt looked at his very masculine facial features and immediately liked what he saw. The man was handsome in a rugged sort of way. His smiling, blue eyes did not disguise the intelligence and capable nature of the man; they positively enhanced it. He looked around at his people gathered there, a smile of pride and conviction on his face; a smile that revealed his great affection for his people. A smile that was wholeheartedly trustworthy.

## Chapter 7

# The Challenge

The sound of contented people pervaded the clearing as Robin and Marion began eating their food. John told the boys that Robin would speak afterwards.

"'Tis always better to speak to people with a full belly when there are plans afoot for the Sheriff of Nottingham. People have died in their struggle against tyranny and every attack on the Sheriff and his men brings that risk. Nobody refuses to play their part here, such is the strength of their belief in what they are trying to achieve."

The boys nodded in understanding but could not help feeling worried about the part they might be expected to play.

After the meal, Robin stood upon his tree, raising his hand for silence. He waited patiently for everyone to finish their conversations and then spoke clearly and confidently with the air of one who had complete control.

"Welcome, my friends! Let us commence our meeting. Who has business that needs to be addressed? Stand and be recognised!"

Several men and women stood silently, waiting to be called upon and the chance to voice their issues. One by one they were called and given the opportunity to speak. Robin was obviously held in great esteem as they all addressed him as 'My Lord'. Some spoke of petty grievances, others about new ideas or plans to improve things within the settlement. In each case, Robin opened their problems to the people for discussion. He never solved or decided on the issues himself but allowed the group to be self-governing. John explained to the boys about Robin's belief in a fair and open society.

When all those standing had been heard, Robin raised his hand again and asked to be introduced to any newcomers to the group. Matt and James were told to stand, along with four other men who were also new to the group. One by one they were asked to state their names, where they came from and what they could contribute to the community. James and Matt were the last to be called.

"Who invites these two men to our camp?" asked Robin, warmly.

John Little rose from his seated position.

"'Tis I, Robin!" he said in a loud voice.

"I have heard of these men's great strength that would be useful in our encounters with the Sheriff's men," said Robin with a twinkle in his eyes. "Tell me how thou first met them, John Little."

A few people started laughing; it was clear that Robin already knew the details and John turned a little darker in colour as he relayed the details without mentioning the pool incident.

"I heard tell rather more than that," persisted Robin. "Was there not a bathing incident as well?" There was more laughter from the crowd. "Pray, spare not the details!"

Robin was clearly teasing his friend, but Matt suddenly

felt embarrassed for John; he had been really good to James and him since they had arrived in camp, and he wanted to spare John some of the ridicule being directed at him.

He spoke out loudly and clearly.

"My good friend's dip was caused by my clumsiness, my Lord. As I lost my footing, I pulled James into the pool. Little John tried to help me out, but I slipped on a rock and pulled the unfortunate man in too."

There were a few chuckles from those knowing the real turn of events.

"I do not believe mine ears," said Robin. "Finally, John Little has met his match, but indeed the two who are now being celebrated for their part strive to save him from our merriment! I know, John, that thou canst be most persuasive, but verily thou art to be commended! Sit down, my friend – there will be no more laughter at thine expense!" He grinned at John warmly and John was able to relax again.

"So, Matthew Smith," continued Robin. "What canst thou offer our community? What talents have thee to better our life here?"

"I am a blacksmith – I can offer my services making tools and weapons."

"We can never have enough blacksmiths, especially with the plans that I shall share with ye anon," said Robin. "Who will vouch for this man?"

Andrew, the smith they had met earlier, got to his feet and announced his support, then John stood and added his.

"I see that the bond between ye works both ways," he said, warmly. "Welcome to our community, Matthew Smith."

The crowd cheered as they had with the initiation of the previous newcomers.

"And what about thee, James Thatcher? What skills can thou offer us?"

James spoke out confidently.

"I am a thatcher, my lord, as my name suggests, and I would offer my services as such."

"Thou mayest well be using thy skills in a different way than thou art used to, James Thatcher! Who will vouch for this man?"

James cringed. So far he had not met anybody who had appeared to know him as Matt had. But then a man and a woman towards the rear of the clearing stood.

"We do, Robin! The Sheriff's men killed his parents and put him out of business many years ago when he was but a boy. It pleases us to see he fares well."

John Little stood again, but before he could speak, Robin acknowledged him, saying, "I expected that thou wouldst speak for him too, John Little. Welcome to our community, James Thatcher!"

This was again greeted with cheers by the crowd, and Robin had to raise his hands once more to be able to continue.

As he waited patiently for silence to prevail, an air of excited anticipation spread throughout the clearing; this was the time when Robin would announce a new scheme to relieve the Sheriff of more of his ill-gotten gains.

"My friends…" Robin started, in a more serious tone. "I now bring ye plans for our most daring attack yet on the Sheriff of Nottingham. If successful, we will collect enough treasure to pay King Richard's ransom and thus secure his return to England."

He paused to let the crowd cheer and waited for silence to return before he continued. "This plan is so audacious that, for now, I shall not give more details than strictly necessary," he said, to which the crowd gave a low collective moan of disappointment.

"This is so bold," he continued, "that secrecy must be at the forefront of all our minds. Suffice it to say that we shall undergo great risk and, indeed, may incur some loss from our number. 'Tis imperative that we keep this risk to a minimum. The treasure we seek will be passing through the western edge of Sherwood Forest in just two weeks' time, and will be guarded by a small army of the Sheriff's men. That gives us but little time to prepare for this raid.

"Our first priority will be to forge new weapons and train ourselves for battle. We will reduce the risk to us by fighting 'the Sherwood way' as much as we can. However, realistically, taking on the enemy in such numbers would suggest that this will have but a limited effect."

The crowd started to buzz excitedly, and Robin paused for the animated discussion to die down before raising his hands once more.

"I will speak to each group of tradesmen tomorrow about the preparations required of them. These details must remain secret from all others to allow maximum secrecy for our mission. If any of us are captured during this period of preparation, we will be able to reveal but little of our plans, even under torture. I would ask that anybody planning to leave the forest postpone their journey. We have food enough here for this period and I will not risk losing a single man. Every man here will train for four hours each day in a battle skill most suited to them, including the tradesmen; thou canst arrange shifts to ensure production is continued.

"Women can train with the bow. I will have smaller bows constructed than the usual longbows which they can more readily handle. Ye will fight from a distance to support your men; we need as many hands to the task as possible. What we attempt here is not without risk, but t'will bring great reward to those who come through. With good planning, our losses will be minimal. If we achieve our goal, I promise ye this: when the ransom for our king has been paid and he returns, ye will all be able to leave Sherwood as free men. My own estates are vast, and when they are rightfully returned to me, each of ye shall have a piece that you can call your own, where ye can lay the foundations for the future of your children and your children's children. Hear this pledge I give ye, and know that 'tis given by an honourable man!" Robin finished, to a crescendo of cheering and chanting.

Marion, having sat for so long beside Robin, beamed her radiance upon all who looked in her direction.

Matt and James looked at each other with grins on their faces.

"This is going to be some adventure," said James, as excited as any of the crowd.

"That's for sure!" responded Matt with equal exuberance. "I wonder if I'll remember that speech – it'd go down a treat in my homework."

Robin started mingling amongst the crowd with Marion attentively by his side. They moved slowly, pausing to talk to every man and woman, knowing each by name. Even the children were spoken to, their hair often being ruffled affectionately. Slowly, they moved towards Matt and James who stood politely to meet them.

"He who can land John Little in a pond in a fair fight is worthy of shaking my hand," said Robin, the amusement at the thought of this clear to be seen. "I wish I had been there to bear witness to the act!"

John raced to his feet in indignation.

"Forgive my amusement at your expense, John, but I have waited a long time for this to pass," said Robin, beaming his most charming smile at John who held his arms up in mock defeat.

"Perhaps 'tis time *we* had a friendly bout to see which of us would end up in the pond," said John with a wicked grin on his face.

Robin laughed delightedly and slapped his friend on the shoulder.

"There will be time enough for that when all this is over," he replied, accepting the challenge.

He turned to Matt and James and offered them his hand. Both shook it warmly and felt the penetrating force of the eyes that looked directly into their own. Neither backed away from the look and Robin slapped them on the shoulder in the same manner as he had John's.

"Do ye have fighting skills?" he enquired.

"Not really, but we are prepared to learn," answered Matt, eagerly.

"James displayed no little ability with the longbow, Robin, and they both have a most singular way of fighting at close hand," John told him.

"So I hear. Little escapes my attention here, and I desire to hear the particulars when we have more time at liberty," replied Robin, eager to have another opportunity to poke fun at his friend.

"James, I would like thee to practise with the bow

from this day forth. And Matthew, I wish for another man to train in close-quarter combat. Two weeks is too short a time to teach thee skills with the sword, but thou hast shown great strength already and perhaps thou couldst train with John and a staff."

Matt and James promised that they would do their best and Robin replied that was all he ever wanted of his men. Then he was gone, continuing his dialogues with other men in his band.

John left to sort out a battle between his two eldest sons, leaving them alone for a while.

"We've just spoken to Robin Hood!" exclaimed Matt, adrenaline flowing even at the thought of what was to come.

James nodded – he looked thoughtful.

"You realise that we may be asked to fight to the death, James?" said Matt, with a more serious look on his face.

"That's just what I was thinking about. Fighting, I'm prepared to do. But killing is not something I wish to partake in," replied James, equally seriously.

"Even if somebody is trying to kill you?" persisted Matt.

"There's no way that I'm going to kill anybody. There must be another way and I'll think of it. Killing somebody, even if they're an out-and-out villain, is as bad as being one of them. Besides," he added, "what would our parents do if anything happened to us? They don't even know where we are! This is getting way too heavy. Thank goodness they don't have guns!"

"My friend, you worry too much. Nothing's going to happen to us – just sit back and enjoy the ride!" Matt let the matter drop for the moment. He knew that when James dug his heels in, there was little anyone could do to change his mind. "I wonder where we're going to sleep tonight?" he said, deliberately changing the subject.

He saw John returning towards them, knowing that he would get the answer to that and anything else he needed to know, from the giant figure who had clearly taken a liking to both of them.

Chapter 8

# Preparations

They slept outside that night, lying on their backs and getting the occasional glimpse of a star twinkling through the canopy, as they drifted off into an exhausted but peaceful slumber. They were woken at first light by John, who led them to the small stream to wash. The water refreshed them and fortified them for the unknown day ahead. The boys felt the excitement coursing through their veins; they knew that they would go their separate ways today, each starting their training at their respective places, before joining their fellow tradesman for an afternoon of labour. Both felt confident about the training session but were apprehensive about the work they would have to undertake. Matt had suggested that they would instinctively know what to do, as they had the day before, but his confident suggestion merely covered his own concerns.

Heather brought them a hunk of bread and some slices of cheese for breakfast which they washed down with fresh, cool water from the stream.

John asked if James could remember the route to the archery training area, and then sent him on his way with the offer of a meal at midday, when he responded affirmatively. Then he motioned to Matt to follow him and led the way to the close-quarter training area.

"I want thee to show how thou downed me yesterday and took the wind from my belly. Until I had my breath back, I was as much use as a baby. This trick could rid us of the 'tailers' before the battle doth commence," explained John.

"Tailers! What are tailers?" asked Matt, attentively.

"When an army marches, few have the privilege to ride on horseback. When we encounter the Sheriff's men, excepting the knights leading them, the most part will travel afoot. They become strung out over a distance, oft with many yards between pairs of soldiers. Those at the rear are the weakest travellers over any long distance and are known as the 'tailers'," John informed him. "Thy method of fighting would remove the tailers before we get into battle. Imagine a narrow path with our men concealed in the bushes. Then, as the tailers pass, two men surprise them and bring them down. I could scarce utter a sound when thou knocked the breath out of me. When they are brought down, we drag them to the bushes and truss them up. Two men fewer to battle against!"

"How many men do you think we will be fighting, John?" asked Matt.

"If the treasure is as plentiful as Robert suggested, mayhap a hundred or more. We can match the number but cannot compete with the power of the Sheriff's weaponry or armour. We need to fight with our wits as much as our might," finished John, as they arrived at the fighting area.

There was already a small gathering of about fifteen men, and more were arriving by the minute for the session led by John himself. All the men were heavily built and had been handpicked for close-quarter fighting.

John paired the men up and gave each pair a wooden practice sword, crudely cut but perfect for training. For the first activity, the swordsmen were to swing their swords at their partners, simulating battle. The partners were supposed to dodge the blows and grab the sword arm to prevent it being swung. At the same time, they were to use their feet to bring the swordsmen down by wrapping their foot around one leg and pushing either forwards or backwards. From there they were to disarm the sword.

Matt excelled at this, his concentration as intense as it would have been in a rugby match. After a while, it became clear that he was one of the best, so John decided to test him on himself. Matt grinned at him in anticipation, knowing that John might use this opportunity to get his own back.

John, seeing the grin, knew immediately what Matt was thinking.

"Do I see a look of fear upon thy face?" he taunted.

Matt wasn't worried at all. He knew he had the element of speed on his side and intended to use it to his advantage. John swung the wooden sword above his head and started to bring it down hard towards Matt's shoulder. Matt skipped easily to the side, leaving the sword swooping down futilely. In a split second he had ducked back in, grabbing John's arm while he was still off-balance, forcing it forwards and making John lean over further. At the same time he pushed his foot between John's and twisted it, locking it behind one of his ankles. Then, instead of pushing him backwards as John had been expecting, he tugged hard at the sword arm and John went sprawling forward. Matt picked up the fallen sword and placed it at John's throat.

"You did not fight as we practised – you pulled instead of pushing!" he exclaimed, indignantly. "I was not to expect that!"

"That's the point, John. You've been watching me all morning; if I had put into practice what you were expecting, your strength would easily have countered anything I had to offer. Once you've done this in battle a few times, the enemy would notice the style and compensate, as you were ready to do. The need to vary the technique is crucial for success."

John nodded; he understood only too clearly the implications that Matt was making.

"That is the last time thou throwest me to the ground," he muttered to himself, but just loud enough for Matt to hear. Matt raised his eyebrows in amusement as he met John's gaze. John instructed the rest of the group to try Matt's new approach, and the rest of the morning passed quickly by.

They headed back to John's for lunch, which Heather served them as soon as they arrived. They ate in silence, before spending half an hour discussing other strategies that could be used to outmanoeuvre the enemy. John showed a real interest in the flying tackles that Matt and James had used on him the day before, and Matt promised to teach him these the following day.

After this, Matt made his own way to the noisy blacksmith's area, where he found a number of men already hard at work, pounding their hammers on red-hot metal.

Andrew, the smith who had spoken for him yesterday, noticed his arrival and offered him a heavily gloved hand to shake. Matt thanked him for speaking on his behalf the previous day.

"We are making swords today and have organised the men into teams, each taking one part of the process. The space we have to work in here is limited, as are the fires and tools we use. I think you would be best-placed shaping the blade with a hammer. I have men to beat the metal flat, but few have the skill of thy father for detailed work; I am hoping he has passed his skills to you," he told Matt.

Matt, secretly concerned that his inexperience was to be revealed to them all, nevertheless responded positively and asked what techniques they were using. He hoped that he would at least be shown a demonstration to give him some idea as to how to achieve this stage of the swords' manufacture.

Fortunately, Andrew appeared encouraged by his question, and took him along each stage of the production line. Matt watched each man carefully but concentrated particularly hard at the shaping stage.

The man he was to replace was heavy-handed with the hammer and by the time he had fashioned the shape of the blade, it was necessary to return it to the previous stage to be flattened once again. This, in turn, meant that the process of shaping needed additional work too. As the blade went back along the line, the man apologised for his lack of skill to Andrew.

"I beg your pardon. Though I am improving, I am no natural at this."

Andrew accepted the apology readily and reassured him that even the best blacksmiths in the world were inexperienced to start with. He explained to Matt that the fellow was a farm labourer before joining Robin's men and had had no previous training as a blacksmith. Calling him out of the line, he took the man's hammer and gloves.

"Take a break and help keep the fires stoked. Let us see what Matthew can do," he told him, to the man's evident relief. Then he handed the gloves to Matt who put them on his own hands, flexing his fingers against the stiffness of the thick leather. He took the hammer and the man next to him passed over a length of flattened, red-hot metal. He made tentative hits to the metal at first, unsure of how hard to hit the metal. Andrew voiced his approval of the way that Matt tested the weight and balance of the hammer. Matt nodded and started to hit it harder, working his way down the length of one side and then the next. As he hammered, the sword began to take shape until, with a grunt of pleasure, he held it up to show Andrew, who grinned at him and walked away, leaving him to carry on unsupervised.

After an hour he took a break with his fellow smiths, chatting easily with them. He learned much about his new job and the different stages involved, and even managed to spend a little time with the old man who was carving oak handles to fit the swords. Each handle was drilled out with a hand awl to slide on to the metal end of the sword, before being scraped and shaped smooth with what was little more than a penknife. Matt admired the old man's technique and even made time to try it for himself. He was surprised how labour intensive it was and soon gave up and returned to his shaping duties.

As the light started to fade that evening, he returned to John's dwelling exhausted, with aching muscles and covered in black soot but with a pleasant feeling of satisfaction. He had achieved much today; made new friends, learned new skills and gained respect from the people he had associated with.

Heather met him as he flopped down exhaustedly where they had eaten the previous night. "God's teeth, look at the state of thee! Thou shalt be going to wash at the stream before thou eats at my table tonight," she told him, firmly but with a grin on her face. "Worked thee hard, did they?"

He nodded, saying that he needed to work extra hard to be able to cope with the amount of food she gave him. She took the compliment with a smile of pride and went back inside, returning shortly with a rough bar of soap and a piece of coarse cloth.

"Thou mayst run into John at the brook; I sent him off a short while since, though he was not as filthy as thee! He may try to give you a dip tonight, I hear thou dumped him on his backside again today, so he may be looking for revenge when thou least expects it," she said, laughing. "'Tis about time somebody gave him his comeuppance, the big oaf!"

Matt pulled himself wearily to his feet and headed down to the stream.

There were many men there in various states of undress, washing the filth of a long day from their bodies. Matt saw John talking to Andrew and went to join them.

"Sounds like thou hadst as good an afternoon as your morning," John offered, generously. "I heard tell of your skills from the goodly Andrew. Apparently, the rate of production went up to its highest yet today, with such quality! Good man! It makes me glad that we spoke up for thee."

Matt murmured his thanks, looking a little embarrassed at the praise, and started to strip off his shirt. It was difficult to build up lather with the crude soap, but he washed and rinsed off in a small pool. As the pool cleared from the disturbance he had caused, his reflection came into view and he stared at the image that emerged, his mouth falling open in surprise. He could not take his eyes from the image reflecting back at him – for it was not his own...

## Chapter 9

# James Makes His Mark

James had left Matt and John, and made his way to the archery area. He was unsure of what to expect and hoped that he could hold his own with the more experienced archers. As he approached, he was greeted by the man who had watched him shoot yesterday. Thomas' greeting was formal but warm, and he was introduced to some of the others in the group. Thomas took a crossbow from a small heap of weapons scattered by an old alder tree and handed one to James. James felt its weight, juggling it in his hands trying to make it feel comfortable. Thomas watched him carefully.

"Thou hast not used one before, hast thou?" he asked.

James shook his head.

"No, but I'm willing to give it a go."

Thomas showed him how to hold it correctly and how to load it. He pointed to a stout tree about twenty paces away and gave the bow back to James who, after a moment's hesitation, took aim and fired. His arrow hit the tree exactly where he had intended it to. Thomas nodded his approval and then shot an arrow which landed about a foot away from the first but at the same height.

"Now shoot one between the two," he instructed, so James reloaded and took aim again. His bolt landed at the right spot but about two feet too high. He tried several more bolts, listening to the advice that Thomas gave him but without much success.

"This is clearly not thy preferred weapon, we will practise with the longbow next," Thomas told him.

James had shown aptitude for this the previous day and was looking forward to trying it again. A tree was selected fifty yards away and Thomas used a piece of chalky stone to mark out a square target about a foot wide. As they walked back to the firing positions, Thomas set out clear expectations based on what he had seen James achieve yesterday. Thomas himself fired the first three arrows, making a small grouping towards the centre of the target.

James, having watched Thomas' technique carefully, drew an arrow and aimed at the target. He fired and the arrow embedded itself into the top left of the target.

"Thine aim is slightly out," said Thomas, disappointment edging into his voice.

James said nothing, loaded and fired a second arrow. This time his arrow hit the top right corner of the target. "Thou art correcting too much. That was too high," Thomas told him. "Relax thy shoulders and flex thy knees when thou shoots."

Again James reloaded, and fired two arrows in quick succession. His arrows hit the bottom left and then the bottom right corners of the target. Then he drew a fifth arrow and sent it into the centre of the square.

Thomas looked at him with respect. "Thou knewest exactly what thou wert doing, didst thou not? That is fine shooting, lad," he said and clapped James none too gently on the back.

"Clearly, this is my preferred weapon!" said James,

with a proud grin on his face. "Wouldn't you agree?"

A voice from behind them broke their conversation.

"There are few archers in Sherwood that accurate!"

James turned to see the Hood standing behind them, his arrival unannounced.

"I heard tell of thy skill with the bow and came to establish if the rumour held true," said Robin, easily. "It would appear that what I heard was accurate. Art thou willing to face a challenge? It has been a long time since I faced an opponent with such ability."

James nodded, eager to impress, and Robin instructed Andrew to fetch the arrows and mark a smaller target on the same tree. Thomas went off at a run, while the other men stopped their own practice and gathered round.

The target that Thomas marked looked ridiculously small and James wondered just how close he could get to it, scarcely believing he would even be able to hit it.

"How long hast thou used a bow?" Robin asked him.

"My father taught me when I was young. We practised regularly whenever we got a chance, but he was much better than me," James told him.

"He taught thee well. But how didst thou avoid being forced into the Sheriff's army?"

"We practised in private. It was a father-son thing – something we did just for the personal challenge," James answered, thinking quickly on his feet.

"Well, the Sheriff's loss is our gain!" Robin told him enthusiastically. "Wouldst thou like to go first or second?"

"First, I think," James told him, unsure of where the advantage might lie.

Robin nodded and drew back out of James' field of vision. He watched as the young man loaded an arrow and took aim before pulling back the drawstring. The bow automatically lifted as he did so and he compensated by lowering it and taking aim a second time, then letting the arrow fly.

The arrow hit the target area slightly right of centre. There was a ripple of excitement through the crowd as they realised that this was to be a worthy competition. James moved back and allowed Robin to take his place.

Robin's first arrow kissed James' as it buried itself alongside. Again, the group murmured their approval. They fired twice more, each arrow touching another in the tightest grouping anybody had ever seen. Robin instructed Thomas to select a tree at seventy yards and mark a target of a similar size. Then he took two arrows and handed one to James.

"The arrow closer to the centre will be declared the winner," he said, issuing his next challenge.

Robin and James both fired their arrows but, from this distance, it was hard to judge who was closer to the centre. Thomas was dispatched to check the result. Upon his return he pointed to Robin.

"By this distance," he said. He held his finger and thumb apart by the narrowest margin to indicate just how close it had been.

Robin looked at James with respect.

"Perhaps thou wouldst join me and two others on a hunt this morning. The community needs fresh meat and with thy skill and mine, it should not take us long!"

"I would indeed be honoured to hunt with you, Robin," James told him, realising the privilege he had been granted.

A short while later, they set off with Robin leading the

way. James followed just behind and two other men, both butchers by trade, pulled a simple cart behind them. They travelled silently at first, before Robin signalled to James to walk alongside him.

"Thou art a quiet man, James Thatcher. A man who speaks through his actions and skill is rare these days. Already, through thine endeavours, thou hast earned the respect of others, including mine. I wonder if thy skill at thatching matches that with a bow?" he enquired.

James wasn't certain how to answer this; as yet he'd had no opportunity to try out his supposed trade.

"I always do as best I can," he replied, diplomatically.

"Thou art modest as well," replied Robin. "Well, James, I have some ideas with which thou might be able to help me. Ideas that could help us swing the tide of battle in our favour.

"Imagine, if thou wilt, the enemy walking along a narrow path through Sherwood Forest. Everything appears quiet – peaceful even. As the tail end passes, a man from either side of the trail appears like magic. In silence, they disarm the last two men, before disappearing back into the forest, again without making a single sound. A succession of such events could greatly reduce the number of soldiers we have to fight in the main battle."

"The idea is good, but where would I fit in?" James asked him.

"To hide in the forest means appearing as part of the forest. What I would like thee to do is construct some lightweight thatched covers, not much deeper than a span. These can be concealed with branches. Position these over holes about a cubit deep, and ye could conceal two men beneath. The men who wait here will also be covered with branches and leaves to conceal them. These will be the men whom thy friend instructs in his singular way of fighting. The force of the 'tackles' should drive each soldier into holes on the opposite side, where they can be restrained without effort. The covers will come down and, lo, the soldiers have magically disappeared from the forest. If our men are unseen, it will add to the fears of men who believe this forest is haunted and unsettle the legion further. What say ye?"

James could not help himself from grinning at the ingenious plan.

"I like it, I really like it! But if you want to reduce the numbers of the enemy greatly, we are talking about a lot of traps and a lot of our forces being tied up. Two of us for every one of them. Are there enough men for this and for the main battle?"

"Unfortunately, there are not. In each case, the men in the holes will have to truss up their captives and return to join the main force deeper in the forest."

"What number are we expecting to fight?"

"The numbers are fairly evenly balanced. I estimate about one hundred and twenty on each side. The real problem is that my men do not have the armour or quality of weapons. The more of the enemy we can eliminate from the main battle, the better we will fare. I plan to relieve the Sheriff of Nottingham of more of his men by ambushing groups that are too big for the assault teams. If all goes well, by the time we get to the main battle, there will be so few of the enemy that they will surrender without a struggle."

"You have thought this through carefully. Do you know the route they will take?" asked James.

"There is but one."

"I would want to construct the covers close to where the traps are to be set. The amount of thatching materials I will need is considerable; it makes no sense bringing it to the centre of Sherwood and then having to transport it back. In doing this, each cover will benefit from having the right camouflage for its surroundings," James suggested.

"There is another problem, also. I have but one other thatcher here, which means much work for the two of ye. Ye will need to start to work immediately."

James nodded, the first sign of concern showing on his face.

"I have an idea that might work. The process for making the covers is simple compared to thatching roofs. If I could have a small team of women, I'm sure that they could help in constructing and camouflaging the covers."

"I had not considered using the women for this! I will ask for volunteers when we return," said Robin, finishing the conversation, and silence prevailed amongst the small group.

Before long, they picked up a fresh deer trail leading into some deep forest.

"There are several animals that travel together, Robin," one of the others informed him. Robin nodded and changed his style of walking, bringing each foot down quietly from the outer edge until flat. James copied his technique and soon discovered how effective this was at reducing the noise they made. Robin's keen eyes soon picked up movement ahead and he stilled the group. Testing the gentle breeze with his finger, he nodded his approval and started to walk even slower towards them.

At fifty yards, he stopped and asked for his bow. James was given one too and Robin instructed him to shoot at the animals to the rear of the group while he would take the lead animals.

As James focussed his eyes on the distant creatures, he counted six deer. He had never killed an innocent creature before but knew that the forest dwellers needed to eat. He consoled himself that animals were slaughtered for food in his own world and bit his lip with renewed determination. He loaded an arrow and took aim, releasing his arrow a split second after Robin's. They shot again, but the small herd of deer had disappeared before they were able to load for a third time. The two butchers took the cart and went ahead, while Robin and James took their time. As they approached, the butchers were already about their work and they could see that they had each downed two of the beasts. Robin looked at them and grunted with satisfaction.

"All clean kills. Good shooting, lad!"

"You too, Robin," James answered, not being able to hide his regret at what he had just done.

"'Tis the sign of a good, decent man who shows remorse for killing anything," Robin told him. "I too feel it, and will ask for forgiveness when I pray tonight."

James watched the butchers bleed the animals but refrained from offering to help with the ritual gutting that followed. They finished quicker than James expected and, even though the sight of their craft was a little grisly to him, he watched the experienced men with some respect.

Soon after, Robin announced it was time to return to the community and the men travelled homewards in quiet companionship.

## Chapter 10

# Battle Plans

James returned to John's dwelling to find Matt sitting outside. His friend raised his hand in greeting and stood up.

"I've been waiting for you," he said. "I want to show you something."

"What's the matter? Is there a problem?" he asked, alarmed at the seriousness of his friend's voice.

"Come to the stream to wash, there's something you have to see."

James followed him to the pool where Matt had earlier made his discovery.

"Lean over the water," instructed Matt.

James did as he was requested, pulling back immediately with a gasp, before slowly leaning forward again. "Good grief – so that's what look I like here!" he said with a chuckle.

"It's how everybody sees you – except me, of course."

James leaned over once more and Matt followed suit. They studied each other's reflections in the water. James suddenly started laughing.

"What's so funny?" Matt asked.

"You! Just look at yourself!" said James, laughing harder.

"Perhaps you should take a better look at yourself. You're not so pretty either," said Matt, indignantly.

James took another look and made a face as he observed the dark beard on his chin, the weathered complexion from exposure to sun and wind, and a long scar on his forehead that disappeared into his hairline. He touched it thoughtfully, turning his head this way and that. He had no way of knowing how he had got it but assumed it was to do with his thatching trade. Climbing roofs was not without its risks.

Next, he examined Matt's reflection more closely. He did look like Matt, but at least ten years older. He too looked as though he'd lived a tough life; his nose had obviously been broken at some point, as it was flattened and had an unnatural bend in the middle. Knowing his friend's propensity for finding trouble, he sensed there might also have been the occasional fight, in which someone had not been quite so willing to forgive his exuberant sense of humour.

"No wonder we fit in so well here – we look just like them, just years older than we really are," said Matt.

"Yes, it's definitely us, but I don't think I'd have recognised either of us in a photo."

"It's as if we've taken on the identities and skills of other people, at least to everybody here, although we still see ourselves as us. Boy, this is turning out to be some adventure!" Matt concluded. "Oh, you'd better wash while you're here. Heather has threatened not to feed us if we're dirty and we can't exactly pop round to McDonald's for a quick bite instead!"

"There's something else too, I've been thinking about it for a little while now," James said, before pausing, deep in thought.

"Spit it out then, we haven't got all day."

"It's just that we're teenagers, right? Young *modern* teenagers – we *talk* like teenagers! And yet, apart from John Little's comment when we first met, nobody seems to notice that very much when we talk to the adults around here."

"So you reckon we not only look different and have skills that we shouldn't really have, but we must *sound* like adults to them too? It makes sense, but you don't sound any different to me."

"We don't look any different to each other either."

On the way back they exchanged the stories of their day, each surprised and pleased at how the other had fared with the day's demands.

"Heather told me that Friar Tuck is due to arrive tonight, with information about forthcoming events. Apparently, his visits are always a social event due to the amount of ale he brings with him. Food is to be shared in the gathering area again tonight so that everyone might benefit from his generous offerings," Matt told James.

"Sounds like an excuse for everyone to get drunk, if you ask me!" said James with a grin.

"I had some of my dad's homebrew once – it didn't take much to make me feel pretty rough the next morning. It might be a good idea not to drink too much of this ale," suggested Matt. "Although I don't suppose there'll be any Coke as an alternative. I hope the food'll be ready soon – I'm starving!"

"Me, too!" agreed James.

They arrived back at the camp just as John and his family

had started to make their way to their favourite spot at the meeting area.

"I hear thou hadst a good day with the bow, lad!" said John warmly, slapping James on the back, and none too gently. James grinned at him with a brief nod but didn't comment on his success. As he sat, he wondered how it was that John knew so much about what went on, and how he learned it so quickly. As soon as they were sitting down, Heather offered them another huge helping of food, rivalling yesterday's in quantity. Somehow, this time it did not seem as daunting as before and both boys polished it off effortlessly, only to find their bowls filled once more by the ever-solicitous Heather.

Robin and Marion made their appearance later than the previous night. They were followed by the largest man that Matt and James had ever seen, dressed in a long brown robe that enveloped him from neck to foot. A length of rope held it firmly against his protruding stomach and a large wooden crucifix hung from his neck. It could only be Friar Tuck! He didn't sit on the fallen tree as Robin and Marion did but leant against it. They were deep in conversation and, for once, Robin did not greet the crowd as he usually did. John commented on this, telling the boys that they were probably discussing the forthcoming engagement with the enemy that Robin had spoken of the previous evening.

Huge barrels of ale appeared beside a tree to the left of the Friar, and he motioned a couple of men to share it out. A rough queue quickly formed as people crowded round with their tankards to share the bounty, and John sent one of his sons with three tankards to join it.

"The Friar's ale is the best there is," he informed Matt and James, the anticipation of it clear in his face. The people were enjoying the relaxed gathering and knew that Robin would eventually address them with the news that Friar Tuck brought with him, and nobody seemed to worry that this was taking much longer than normal.

When Robin eventually stood up on his tree, a hush immediately descended upon the gathering. Matt and James sensed the change and looked up expectantly.

"Friends, I trust the liquid refreshment brought by our goodly friend, Friar Tuck, is a suitable reward for the day's labour! Drink up and enjoy, for we have troublesome times ahead...

"Preparations for our forthcoming venture have been set in motion, and already I have seen the changes to our training schedule and, indeed, to our very determination that will lead to our being considered worthy opponents for the Sheriff's army. Whilst I have initiated these changes and laid down expectations in some areas of preparation, there is still much to organise. The good Friar has brought news of developments from Nottingham, which can only be described as 'inside information', and must remain undisclosed, except to the council of leaders who will be advised after this evening's festivities. However, I can inform ye all that the forces we shall be up against are considerable and are being led by the Sheriff's own cousin, Guy of Gisborne. Needless to say, his reputation as a brutal and merciless leader is well-established and must not be taken lightly. He will torture and kill at whim. His presence also threatens a considerable increase in the number of cavalry soldiers we might encounter, which will be harder for us to deal with."

There were murmurs in the crowd as he announced this, and he paused to wait for the noise to subside before continuing.

"I have been in consultation today with members of our group, and already, strategies are being determined that will significantly reduce the losses we may have to endure. Since these discussions, I have made a vow, and I repeat this to ye now, that we shall win the battle and seize the treasure without the loss of a single life!"

Again, excited chattering broke out amongst the crowd and Robin sat down. For now, he had said enough; he wanted time for his thoughts to be absorbed and discussed before he met with the council of leaders.

John grinned at Matt and James. "Trust Robert to come up with something like this! Imagine taking on an army of soldiers and beating them without a single loss of life. Only Robert!" he said, chuckling at the idea.

"You think it's possible then?" asked Matt.

"If Robert says it can be done, then I have no doubt," answered John.

"May I ask why you call him Robert and not Robin like everybody else?" James asked.

"Respect and gratitude, James. Robert has given me more than anybody else ever has. He has given me friendship, trust, freedom and something yet even more precious – the gift of hope. If that isn't a good reason for showing him the courtesy of calling him by his Christian name, then I don't know what is!"

"True gifts indeed," stated James, in understanding.

"After the gathering comes to an end, the council of leaders are to meet. I am one of them and I have been asked to invite ye both to the meeting," John told them.

"Us? What could he possibly want with us? He hardly knows us." responded Matt, bemused.

"Be that as it may, he definitely wants ye to come and I would say that 'tis quite an honour to be asked. Ye will come, will ye not?" John asked them.

"Of course we'll come. It's the least we could do after the hospitality and friendship we've been shown," said James, putting any uncertainty that John may have been feeling to rest.

The Friar's ale ensured that the gathering would last well into the night and that many would suffer from sore heads the following day. There was a celebratory atmosphere and children were allowed to stay up with the adults and join in the spontaneous singing and dancing that took place when the ale flowed and Harold, the lute player, was prevailed on to play for them.

At a signal from Robin, the council of leaders stood up and started to gather. John led the boys down the path towards the houses to another structure, not far from his own. It was brightly lit by oil-filled lamps and they walked into a large space furnished only with a long wooden table with benches placed strategically around it. John motioned them to take a seat. As they sat down, the door opened and three other men came in; John introduced Will Scarlett, John Miller and Henry Talbot. He kept the introductions brief and the six of them sat in relative silence until the door opened again and Robin, Marion and the Friar entered, the Friar only just fitting through the opening. Robin shook hands with them all, while Marion spoke a greeting to each in turn.

"Welcome my friends! I will explain immediately why

I have invited Matthew and James to this meeting. It has been noted that Matthew has some unusual fighting tactics that we can learn to use in our forthcoming venture, and James has undertaken special tasks from me that will have a profound influence on the outcome of that same venture. I realise though, that these two men are very new to our group and that the issue of trust here is questionable. I, along with John Little, speak for both these men, despite how little is known about them and despite the fact that they have yet to earn our trust. The importance of our venture is so keen that I am prepared to take that chance. I request that both of ye not leave our community here for the two weeks leading to our task."

He looked at Matt and James keenly, waiting for a response. Neither backed down from his gaze and both gave their word that they would do as they had been asked.

Robin then unrolled a map of Sherwood Forest. It showed the major trails through it, the streams that bisected it in places and various clearings. He pointed out the trail that was to be used by Guy of Gisborne, explaining that it was about three miles long and particularly narrow in places. He told them that he was expecting about forty horsemen and anything up to sixty foot soldiers. The exact day the travelling forces would set out was known only by himself and the good Friar. He marked on the map the narrowest parts of the trail where only two soldiers would be able to pass side by side or a single horseman.

"These are the places we shall start to remove the tailers from the convoy," said Robin. He told them that capturing the foot soldiers was not without its difficulties, though these were not insurmountable but that the horsemen posed more of a challenge. He explained to the group his idea of using shallow 'hides' that James would be constructing, and they laughed with delight at his audacity.

The problem then would be the horsemen. How could they reduce the number before they sprung their final ambush? The group pondered this silently before James spoke up suddenly.

"Tarzan!" he exclaimed. The others looked at him in bewilderment.

"Tarzan? What is Tarzan, James?" asked Robin.

Matt looked at James with a puzzled smile on his face, wondering what he was going to say next. They had watched all the old Tarzan films together on DVD a few years ago during the summer holidays, and were even inspired to build their own tree house in his grandmother's garden afterwards. He was most intrigued at how James would explain the fictional film character to Robin and his council – *this should be interesting*, he thought!

Thinking on his feet, James explained that Tarzan was the hero in a story that his mother had told him when he was a child. In the story, Tarzan had been raised in a forest in a far-off land and moved around by swinging from vine to vine high up in the trees. He paused, waiting to ensure that they understood what he was saying, before Robin asked how knowing this could help them. James told them that, although they didn't have vines in the forest, they did have rope which could be suspended high up in the trees for them to swing on. Again, there was little sign of comprehension, so he continued.

"Attacking horse soldiers from the ground is dangerous, but if we swing through the air, we can easily unseat these soldiers. If we use these on the narrow parts of the trail, we could unseat three or four at a time before anybody notices," he finished.

Marion started to chuckle as she understood the simplicity of the idea.

"This pleases me greatly! At this rate the whole army could be reduced to less than twenty strong before they walk into the final ambush. This strategy could make the impossible happen – the desire to win without the loss of a single life becomes more realistic."

Robin nodded, also impressed with James's idea.

"We shall make this happen. Tomorrow James and I shall walk the route and mark the places where this tactic can be employed. Then we shall meet again to discuss the preparations." He called an end to the meeting.

"Quick thinking, James!" said Matt as they walked back to Little John's together. "I thought for a moment you were going to ask if they'd seen the film!"

James chuckled at the thought, but already he was looking forward to tomorrow and spending more time alone with the awesome Robin Hood.

## Chapter 11

# Ambush Trail

Both boys began to feel a certain amount of conflict about the ambush, and had discussed their roles at length. They knew that if they were injured, it could be very serious, especially without the reassurance of a hospital or their families nearby; but as time appeared to stand still once they went behind the waterfall, Matt felt almost invincible.

"Nothing will happen to us," said Matt. "This has to be some kind of alternative reality. Of course we'll come back safe and sound."

James, as usual, was more circumspect. He was missing his parents more than he would admit to his friend and was really worried that if anything *did* happen to them, his parents would never know what had become of them. On the other hand, it was so far removed from their normal lives, he was almost convinced that they were, in fact, in some kind of dream world.

"We might as well make the most of it, for now," decided James. "It's not every day that you get the opportunity to relive history, to play an active role in a story we've grown up with."

They decided to go along with the adventure a while longer, certain that they could always change their minds later and return to their own lives again.

Over the next week, preparations went ahead at full steam. James marked the trail with Robin at suitable places for the ground traps and worked non-stop with a small team to set them up. He was left in charge of the two diggers – two trainee women thatchers – and a third woman who took care of the camouflage. The holes were dug on either side of the trail at about two foot deep and could hold two prone men, while the thatched covers were large enough to overlap on each side. The covers were light and reinforced with thin branches to give them more rigidity. It was a fairly slow process and every bit of daylight was used to ensure maximum production.

Matt, on the other hand, spent his day working the steel in the smithy and training. He had used a low-level cart filled with straw bales to represent a horse and had stuffed clothing attached to a central wooden pole to simulate a rider. After attaching ropes to the trees above for the swinging assailants, the cart was pulled along at walking pace. The assailant's task was to swing down and knock the 'rider' off the bales of straw. At first, the swinging men misjudged the timing and many swung either in front or behind their target. But as the days passed, their accuracy greatly improved, and they swung with such momentum and force that repairs were often needed for the 'rider'.

Towards the end of the first week, Robin took Matt along the trail to show him the narrowest parts where the rope swings would be most effective. Matt dutifully marked each place and returned with a small team of men to attach ropes to the trees. Each rope was tested with a practice swing and knotted at the correct height for an assailant to grip with his feet.

With one week to go, Robin took all the men to the

trail and gave each one a place either on a rope swing or under a thatched cover. Twenty archers were kept for the ambush clearing, and bushes from the woods were cut and placed around the clearing to hide them.

The ambush trail was now ready and the rest of the week was given over to training. Robin was pleased with the preparations and the amount they had achieved in such a short time, and praised the work of Matt and James. But Robin wasn't finished there; he had work for the women too. He organised lengths of rope to be placed at every ambush site to tie up the captives. The women would then be left to guard them while the men left their stations and moved forwards to support the final ambush. There was nothing that Robin Hood appeared to have overlooked.

The night before the ambush, Robin called for a communal gathering and feast. It was at this meeting that he would reveal his plans so that everyone would know the part they had to play. The excitement and anticipation had been building all day, and people made their way to the gathering promptly as if their early presence could make things happen quicker. Robin took his time, however, giving strict instructions that there was to be no drinking that night. When everyone had finished eating, he made his entrance with Marion at his side and took his customary place. He spent the first couple of minutes looking round at his people, pride evident on his face before he finally stood and raised his hands for silence. The tension in the crowd could have been cut with a knife.

"There is little I can say to thank ye for all the endeavours ye have undertaken in the past two weeks but, needless to say, the pride I feel towards everyone is testament to everything ye have done. Without complaint or reservation, ye have toiled for our common cause despite not being versed with the final details of our plan. King Richard will be eternally grateful for the loyalty ye have shown me and, consequently, him. No king could ask for finer subjects and I could not wish for finer friends.

"Tomorrow we risk our lives to secure the treasure that will pay for the king's release. If we are successful, it will need to be taken across the sea, along with the amount we have already procured; a journey fraught with risk and danger. I, myself, will lead this journey and direct a small group of men to protect our hard-won spoils. I shall be asking for volunteers for this next task after our mission here has been accomplished. Those that remain will, therefore, be smaller in number and could themselves be at risk if the Sheriff decides to exact his revenge. There is still much to consider and plan for.

"On the subject of the morrow, I shall now explain exactly how events will unfold. The army will be reaching Sherwood just before midday. By that time, they'll have been travelling for some hours so will be tired and less vigilant, and will be spread out considerably along the narrow track through the forest. Gisborne's tactic is usually to intersperse the foot soldiers with riders, but as his impatience is notorious he will be setting quite a pace and, I suspect, the majority of riders will be at the front. Our plan is to attack the foot soldiers first at the rear of the column, capturing them a few at a time, trussing them up and leaving them under the guard of the women. Once they have been disarmed and tied, they will be placed in the traps with the women sitting on top of the roof-covers, thus preventing any escapes. Each time the men have captured and tied an enemy soldier, they will move through the forest in silence and re-join the path further on, to support the final ambush. 'Tis imperative that all these captures go unnoticed by the enemy, so as not to raise the alarm and increase the risk of an all-out battle. The horsemen need to be taken out individually when they too can be 'removed' without being noticed. Where there are more than two horsemen together, they are to be left alone as the risk to us is too great. Once captured and secured, they will be escorted through the forest to a safe clearing and guarded by a chosen group of men who will also handle the horses. When their numbers have been reduced significantly, our archers will then lead the final ambush of the remaining force when they will see the true show of our numbers. Are there any questions?"

"What shall we do with our prisoners?" a man called out.

"Kill them!" responded another and the cry was taken up by others.

James stood up and caught the attention of Robin who raised his hands for silence.

"There is something thou wishes to say, James?"

James nodded and then spoke out calmly and clearly.

"If we take their lives, we are as guilty as they are. Surely, we are better than that? Have we not proved that we can live in a society that is based on true community, one that treats each citizen with consideration and respect? This will all be for nothing if we act as those whose values we despise. I say we should strip them of their weapons and armour, and send them back to the Sheriff with their tails between their legs!"

There was laughter at this idea and murmurs of agreement.

Robin looked at James and conveyed his respect with a silent nod of approval.

"It will be as James suggests. Many of these soldiers have been forced into service against their will and serve only to feed their families. We should be mindful of this and act with compassion."

This time there were shouts of approval.

Robin told everyone that they would take up position early the following morning, and the formal meeting came to an end.

Business over, Robin circulated, talking to all the groups that had been quickly assembled by the council of leaders. He had a few words for nearly everyone, expressing his confidence in them and thanking them for their past efforts. Marion, looking serene, stayed by his side but talked to the women and children in each group.

James was grouped with the archers, as his main involvement would be in the final ambush. Matt was helping to take out the foot soldiers. Because of his strength and skill at this, he would make multiple attacks moving up the line each time and would be one of the last to reach the final ambush site. Both boys were excited about tomorrow, but each was acutely aware of the danger involved.

Matt was going to treat it like he would a scrum in a rugby match: concentrate, prepare and attack. But for James, this was a different type of battle; he would wait the longest for participation and then, if all went well, he would not even have to fire a single arrow. He was a little disappointed and had decided to ask Robin if he could double up by taking on the swinging rope attacks as well. His request was well-received by Robin and granted.

There was little more to take care of, but the gathering stayed together for longer than usual. Everyone understood the risks they would be taking and it was as though they were gathering strength from all the friends and family that surrounded them. Nobody showed any sign of the fear that they may have been feeling; each man and woman understood the implications of their endeavour and what they stood to gain, both individually and communally. This was it – a chance to secure their freedom, to be able to move around the land without fear of reprisal, capture, torture and even death, and an opportunity to receive a piece of land to call their own. Their faith in Robin was absolute; they knew that everything had been meticulously planned to prevent the risk of casualties, but they also knew that there was no gain in life without sacrifice. The mood was buoyant, a sense of anticipation and excitement swept in waves between the groups gathered together.

Robin continued to mingle, and James noticed that he now moved separately from Marion, allowing her the opportunity to speak more privately with the women. Her serenity, grace and sense of calm brought smiles from whoever she spoke to, but James could see something else as well. She had the same strength of conviction as Robin did, and her belief and fortitude were even more evident than he had noticed before. He heard her tell one group that she herself would be with the women securing their captives and he witnessed the women taking comfort and strength from her simple statement, and the pride they displayed at the thought of being in battle alongside the Lady Marion.

Robin allowed the gathering to continue well into the

evening before returning once more to the fallen tree and raising his hands for attention. The crowd hushed and all eyes turned to him.

"My friends – I hope ye have all eaten your fill and are as ready for tomorrow as ye can possibly be. Tomorrow when we feast, we shall enjoy the Friar's ale once more to celebrate our accomplishments, but for now we must bid each other 'goodnight', for we shall be up early to take our positions. I wish ye all a sound night's sleep and will see everyone on the morrow. I would like to meet briefly with the council of leaders, before ye all depart."

There were many calls of 'Goodnight!' and 'God bless thee, Robin Hood!' as the gathering dispersed. James and Matt made their way to the leaders' meeting with John, whose grin was bigger than a Cheshire cat's.

"'Tis going to be a mighty day tomorrow, lads!" he said, relishing the idea of testing his ample strength against the enemy. The leaders soon gathered together, and Robin gave one or two final instructions. He told them that if he was killed or captured, the first priority was to secure the treasure; after all their plans and preparation, he didn't want everything to be in vain. He had left a will with Marion, giving her ownership of his estate upon his death and granting each man a plot of land after it had been reinstated on King Richard's return. John Little was to take charge of getting the ransom to the King's captors.

With that, the meeting ended with a final shaking of hands, and the leaders went to their beds.

Chapter 12

# Ambush

Matt and James slept little that night; the adrenaline flowing through their bodies denying them the peace of restful repose. Quietly, they had talked well into the night, joined by John for a short while, who was experiencing the same insomnia.

Nonetheless, they were up at first light, and ready to meet the biggest challenge of their lives, along with the rest of the village. After a quick meal the main body of people started to leave their houses and make their way up the ridge leaving behind just a few of the older folk and some women to mind the children. There was a long walk to reach the ambush trail and Robin led them at a considerable pace. The line of people stretched out well over two hundred yards and remained ominously quiet as they snaked their way through the forest along a series of narrow, and sometimes almost indiscernible, animal trails.

Both boys had passed this way many times during the preparation work, and could have found their way in the dark if needed. They also felt disinclined to speak and focussed solely on the journey ahead.

When they finally reached the ambush trail, people would separate into groups and head for their individual positions guided by the leader of each section. Matt and James would separate too, heading in opposite directions, not to meet again until reaching the ambush site. Still viewing it as if preparing for a rugby match, Matt felt a little uncomfortable not to be lining up with his friend as they usually did at kick-off but shrugged off the feeling as he concentrated on his own role. The time passed quickly and they reached the trail sooner than they had expected.

As a complete unit, their number was large, from which everyone drew strength and comfort, but this had dissipated as they separated into smaller groups, and a feeling of vulnerability swept through them.

As Matt's group of ambushers had further to walk than the other groups, he led them swiftly along the trail, to what would be the first ambush site. Approaching the covered holes, he left two men and two women at each one, until he and his final companion took their positions at the last one.

James led his group of men to the tree ropes and also left them in groups of four in a number of places dotted along the trail where the path narrowed significantly.
The last group were the band of archers led by Robin who made their way to the final ambush site, where they found positions hidden amongst the bushes.

Robin had devised a simple system to warn everyone of the enemy's approach. Arrows would be fired along the trail from group to group, until all of the ambushers knew that the attack was imminent. How long the enemy would take to get to the final ambush site would obviously be dependent upon the speed at which they were travelling.

But once warned, Robin's men would lie in wait, prepared, patient and silent, with their senses attuned, ready for the tail end of the enemy procession to arrive, before they moved a muscle and attacked.

Matt was in position alongside the man he was partnering, just inside the forest, while two women sat by the trap cover. His comrade, Alfred, was a burly man just a little taller than himself, who had served in King Richard's army on a previous campaign to the one that resulted in King Richard's capture and being held for ransom. He was as tough as they came and it was he who served as lookout and he who would fire the first arrow warning the others of the army's approach. Alfred had exchanged a few words with Matt during the first hour of waiting but now remained silent, as the time of the army's impending approach drew closer and his keen eyes watched for the tell-tale sign of dust in the distance.

It was not long before his eyes picked out the disturbance above the ground at the foot of some faraway hills. He alerted Matt and waited for the army to approach to about a mile distant before he fired his warning arrow along the path towards the next group of ambushers. They both watched and waited; it was still too early to take to their ambush positions under the thatched covers.

"I count over sixty riders to the front with a similar amount of foot soldiers behind," Alfred told Matt. "But they are not in the positions we expected."

Matt thought quickly. This would make the attack on the foot soldiers easier but more difficult for those attacking the horsemen. So many horses in a tight group meant that the opportunities for picking them off one at a time was greatly reduced. If that was not enough to be concerned about, the number reaching the final ambush site would be a lot greater than they had anticipated, and almost certainly meant that an all-out battle would be the likely outcome.

"We need to inform everybody about this; they must be prepared," said Matt. "Where in the line is the treasure wagon?"

"After the first twenty or so riders," replied Alfred, calmly.

Matt made a decision. "Right, this is what we'll do! You run to the next group as fast as you can, quickly relay the information and tell them to pass it along the trail in the same way. Then you high-tail it back here as quickly as you can to take up your position. Understand?"

The man nodded and sped off up the trail, returning in less than five minutes, just as it was time to hide themselves under the trap covers.

The two women retreated behind bushes twenty yards or so from the traps, where they could watch the action safely before coming forward to guard their captives. Within a minute of their concealment they felt vibrations through the ground as the horses approached.

Matt marvelled at the clarity of the reverberations conducted through the ground, which reached a crescendo as the unsuspecting riders passed by. The sound changed to a higher pitch as the foot soldiers began to pass, and Matt watched patiently through the narrow gap he had created, for the final two soldiers to reach him.

It was as he suspected: the soldiers were stretched out over a greater distance than their mounted counterparts, partly due to the great distance they had marched already but also the ruthless pace set by Guy of Gisborne. Many were moaning and complaining quietly to their comrades as they passed. Matt let the last two soldiers walk by and then lifted his cover. His partner on the other side of the trail did likewise at exactly the same moment. They charged at the tail soldiers, taking them at a low point in their backs and driving the wind from their lungs. The soldiers went down with little more than a grunt and hands were quickly placed over their mouths to prevent further sounds. They were dragged unceremoniously back to the traps and trussed up securely before they had a chance to regain their wind and strength. Gags were placed over their mouths and their weapons removed, before the trap covers lowered once more, concealing their bodies. The two women grinned at the men and planted themselves on the cover doors. Each was armed with a knife and would periodically insert it through the thatched cover and pierce their captive, thwarting any potential thoughts of struggle and escape.

Matt and his partner grinned at the simplicity of their act, then began to move deeper into the forest before changing direction to run parallel with the ambush trail. There were far more traps than men and it was necessary to take up position at a second trap further along the trail. This was risky, for they had to intercept the enemy between the horse soldiers and foot soldiers to reach the next position, and the risk of being seen was increased several fold. Nevertheless, they needed to keep to the agreed plan in order to maximise the chance of success.

By the time they started to head towards the trail again, they knew immediately that they had judged it accurately, as they could hear the sound of horsemen passing by again. They caught a glimpse of the women waiting, hiding behind some bushes. There were more women than men at this stage of the ambush, as it was thought that the horse soldiers would put up greater resistance than their marching counterparts. They were bound to be less tired, having ridden the long route.

There was at least a twenty-yard gap between the rear horseman and the leading foot soldiers, but Matt and his partner could not know that and they took the chance to break cover as soon as the last horseman had passed them. They swiftly climbed into the traps, lowering the covers in just a few seconds and began to wait once more. Their view from here was not as clear as it had been from their first traps and they were going to find it hard knowing exactly when the rear soldiers had passed.

Matt counted them off; sixty in the beginning, twenty traps taking twenty men to here could only mean forty left. He was about to go as the fortieth soldier passed, but suddenly caught sight of another two approaching just in time to check his exit from the trap. He bided his time until they passed, and once again launched himself at an unsuspecting soldier.

Just before he connected to his target his foot slipped on the dusty path and he fell right at the feet of the soldier. At first, being startled, the soldier was slow to react, which at least gave Matt time to get to his knees, but that was as far as he got.

Recovering from his initial shock, the soldier drew his sword and, after grabbing Matt's hair and forcing his head back, laid it across his throat.

Matt felt the blood physically drain from his face as he realised the dire predicament he was in. He started to tremble. There was nothing he could do.

"What art thou doing here, lad?" the soldier asked, and Matt sensed the hostility in his voice.

"I am sorry, I was scared when I saw all you soldiers pass by and was trying to get out of your way, but I tripped and fell." Matt tried a simple excuse.

"Be that as it may, but that is not the question I asked thee, lad. What art thou doing here in Sherwood Forest?" the soldier persisted and pressed harder with the sword, just nicking the skin and shedding the first drop of blood.

Matt's eyes widened instantly at the stinging sensation.

"He's here on business for the Hood." The soldier's question was answered by an unexpected female voice.

Matt couldn't move to see where the voice had come from but recognised it nonetheless.

Turning to look behind him, the soldier caught sight of a formidably built woman. He didn't have time to see anything else though, for she unleashed a fully clenched fist straight to the soldiers chin. He was out cold before his body crumpled to the ground.

"Think you can attack a friend of mine, dost thou?" she said as she stood over the soldier, as if waiting for him to get up so she could hit him again.

"Thank you, Heather. I thought my luck had completely run out. Thank goodness you were manning – or should I say *womanning* – this particular point. Your timing was perfect!" Matt told her gratefully before planting a big kiss on her cheek.

Heather's cheeks turned a bright shade of red at the gesture from Matt. "Be off with thee lad and leave this dumb oaf for me to take care of."

Matt nodded and disappeared back up the trail.

The success of these attacks continued along the trail with each of Robin's men fulfilling their roles admirably, and as a result, Guy of Gisborne's army had been reduced by nearly fifty men.

Matt was aware that there were too few traps for all of the foot soldiers and that there were a dozen or so left. He sent his partner into the woods to intercept a few men who would be racing to the final ambush site and laid a plan to take out the remaining foot soldiers. He was soon joined by eight others and told them of his idea to ambush the rest. They would take them in the same manner as they had so far, but this time they would gag them and secure them to trees, leaving them in the woods while they travelled to the final ambush site.

Once again they travelled through the forest, parallel to the trail, until the sound of horses alerted them to the place they would need to wait. Then Alfred was sent to get an idea of the final numbers. He returned swiftly, saying that he could see fourteen men travelling in three groups; six in the first group and two groups of four behind, with about ten yards between each group. They decided to split up and take out the rear two groups first. Matt sent five men ahead to select a second ambush site before readying himself and three others. The success continued as the two groups captured and secured more of the enemy. It was decided to leave the group of six as they were almost at the interception point for the first horses and their riders, and they did not want to risk alerting their enemy.

The knights were travelling in a much closer formation than expected and although those that waited to intercept them were aware of this, the chance of reducing their numbers quietly was greatly reduced. Matt and his small band headed for the final ambush site as quickly as they could, knowing that the information they carried was vitally important in warning Robin that their final engagement with the enemy would involve a greater number of them.

As they travelled, they met with many of their comrades who had enjoyed similar successful captures, and who were also making their way to the site of the final ambush. So far it had all gone to plan, with almost half of the enemy soldiers taken care of without any serious injury. Matt was really proud of what they had accomplished so far, but he was also aware that the battle was far from over and the likelihood of avoiding the final fight was looking more and more unlikely.

## Chapter 13

# Securing the Treasure?

While Matt was moving towards the site selected for the final show-down, James was stationed up a tall tree, with a long length of rope secured to a stout branch above him, lying across his lap in readiness.

Since the warning arrows had started their lengthy journey along the trail, James had waited impatiently. He knew that his friend had already been involved in the action and longed for the moment when the adrenaline would course through his body too. He had no way of knowing how long Guy's army would take to travel the ambush trail, so all his senses were already on high alert. Like Matt, James had taken up the first strike position, eager for a possible second attempt further up the trail.

The thrumming sound of horse's hooves reached his ears and the long-awaited adrenaline began to flow. He placed his feet above the knot in the rope and applied pressure to grip it, then shuffled his position on the branch so that he was poised to release at a moment's notice. The first of the riders passed by, oblivious to the covert scene around them.

Guy of Gisborne rode fourth in the column, his armour of a better style and quality than that of his riding companions in front and behind him. At last, James caught sight of the carriage, its wheels straddling the complete width of the trail at this point and its contents hidden by a covering of rough cloth. He had counted twenty riders in front of the wagon and knew there were forty more to follow and he patiently counted them off one at a time. The fortieth rider approached him and he was just about to release his grip on the tree, when another came into view. Peering anxiously down the route, he decided that this was definitely the last horseman, and as he drew level he let himself go.

The speed of the swing increased dramatically as he approached the unsuspecting rider and James braced himself for the impact which came with shocking force. The rider flew from his horse and into the bushes on the other side of the trail with James landing squarely on top. Unfortunately for the soldier, his helmeted head hit the base of a small tree trunk with a sickening blow, knocking him unconscious. James quickly tied him up, relieving the man of his weapons, before returning to the trail to fetch the horse, now grazing at the edge of the track. He gathered the reins and walked it further into the forest before slapping it hard on the rump, watching satisfied, as it cantered off.

While James ran through the forest as Matt had done before him, his companions continued to reduce the number of soldiers on horseback. Eight in total had been successfully removed from their horses, before one of the Hood's ambushers misjudged the tail end of the army. Instead of swinging at the last rider in the procession, he had attacked the fourth from the end, removing him from his horse just as the next horseman came into view.

The horseman saw what had happened and called out a warning.

Then there was chaos.

The riders behind the wagon heard the warning and turned their horses to see what was happening. This in itself was difficult at the narrow parts of the trail, and the unfortunate riders at these points impeded those who had turned easily and were riding back down the trail.

The men still left in the trees held their positions, hoping to execute their swings should the opportunity present itself.

James, and the men who had already completed their attacks, had rejoined the trail. Thinking quickly, he positioned himself with another three men on either side of the trail to form another ambush, hoping to be able to take out a small group of cavalry if the opportunity arose. The disorder and confusion amongst the horsemen gradually abated as they began to organise themselves; one of the leaders barked out orders and the group stopped and split into two. Eight riders continued back down the path the way they had all originally come, while the rest turned again and cantered back towards the wagon.

James let the riders pass by as they returned, their numbers and height too great a risk to take on, but as they continued up the trail, six more were taken out by the Hood's flyers. The soldiers who were sent back down the trail soon realised that something was wrong as they met none of the colleagues who had been riding behind them.

Before long they turned again, cantering back towards the wagon in order to warn their fellow soldiers. James had anticipated this, leaving the concealment of the bushes and stood in the middle of the path with the three men. He told the others to remain hidden until the horses had passed by; they were to block the escape route back down the trail. Before long, James heard the sound of the approaching horses and steeled himself. Each of the men took an arrow and loaded their bows. The riders came awkwardly around the slight bend, ducking under some low foliage that stretched from an overhanging branch. The rider pulled up sharply, raising his shield at the sight of the archers, followed shortly by the others.

James stood his ground, saying nothing until the front horseman opened his mouth.

"Who have we here? What business do ye have threatening the royal army?"

"You are no royal army! You will dismount and surrender yourselves now, in the name of Robin Hood," said James quietly but forcefully, showing no fear.

"What makes thee think we shall surrender to a group of common thieves, especially as ye are outnumbered?"

"Take a look behind you, soldier, and see who is outnumbered!"

The man glanced apprehensively behind him and saw four more men standing behind the last of the group. At that moment, the bushes to the side parted and half a dozen more men appeared, led by Matt who grinned at James with amusement.

"I heard the noise and thought you might need a hand, but I see that you have the situation under control," he said to his friend. "If I had known it was you, I would have continued up the trail, but now I'm here, we might as well help secure the prisoners."

The soldiers raised their hands and dismounted,

recognising the futility of their predicament and were promptly disarmed and tied up, with two men stationed as guards.

James quickly told Matt what had happened and informed him that there were still forty or so riders to take care of.

"We must get to Robin quickly! The more men he has with him, the better chance we'll have of preventing bloodshed."

Matt nodded in understanding.

"Can any of you ride a horse?" he asked. Four raised their hands. "The rest of you must get to the final ambush site as fast as you can," he said to the others. They disappeared into the forest and were out of site in seconds.

Matt, James and the four who could ride took the captured horses to ride up the trail at a slow canter. It was not long before they caught up with the two rear horsemen who were a little way behind the main body of cavalry. Matt and James rode up alongside the two unsuspecting soldiers who evidently assumed they were their own comrades, until it was too late.

"Not a good day for a fight, is it?" James asked, pointing his loaded bow at one of them.

The man raised his hands and was encouraged off his horse alongside his riding partner. With two more men secured, they set off up the trail once more.

The next group was significantly bigger, seven or eight riding in close order but along a particularly narrow part of the trail. Even as they drew close, James realised that they were not going to be able to catch these in the same way. Just as he was contemplating his dilemma, a shape flew through the air at speed taking the last rider off his horse and crashing him into the forest. The noise alerted the others who stopped in confusion. Two more shapes flew by and two further riders vanished into the forest, leaving four alarmed and agitated soldiers. Matt and his band rode up quickly, pointing their arrows at the rest of the group who, in their confusion, raised their hands in surrender immediately.

"We need to separate the remaining soldiers at the rear of the carriage, from the carriage itself, if we are to have any chance with the final ambush. There are still about twenty of them left, with a similar amount in front," James told his small group of men.

"There are too few of us to try this strategy again," said Matt.

"What we need is a diversion, something to draw some of the riders away from the group where we can deal with them without risk," mused James.

"What do you suggest?" asked Matt with interest.

"Well, everybody knows that Sherwood is haunted, except for the people who know better! So why don't we give them a haunting?" suggested James. "If we follow them up the trail and start making strange noises and rustle a few bushes as if the place were haunted, we might encourage a few to turn and run or, at the very least, stop and investigate."

Matt laughed at his friend's ingenious idea.

"Let's do it – this really is going to be fun!"

Once again, they left two men guarding the prisoners and sent the others off through the forest to set up an area for the haunting. The six riders kept to the trail and set off in pursuit of the next group of horsemen.

Even though the trail continued to twist and turn, it was not long before Matt spotted the last of the horses behind the wagon. He counted off twenty-two men in total.

Shortly afterwards, strange noises started to emanate from the forest. Long, eerie, banshee-type wails reached James and the small group of riders. Matt stifled a laugh at the convincing noises, as the soldiers drew swords in fear of what they heard but couldn't see. Bushes to the side of the riders started to shake violently, adding to the soldiers' fright. One soldier to the front of the group was not so easily scared, however, and ordered a group of six to investigate.

No sooner had the main group disappeared around a bend than they were intercepted by James' band. They gave up easily and were soon secured. They played the trick once more, successfully catching another group of six before they made plans to take out the remaining ten.

The noise they made had alerted more of Robin's men who were making their way to the final ambush site. They came to investigate and quickly joined up with James. With his numbers now grown to more than twenty, James felt sure they could remove the last of the cavalry soldiers who tailed the wagon. It was merely a case of travelling through the forest once more and laying ambush.

In fact, they were even more successful than anticipated. The front riders had left a distance between themselves and the carriage, and the ambush that Matt and James had set secured both the carriage and soldiers without the need for a fight.

Matt instructed eight of the men to get the loaded cart back to the centre of the forest while the rest made their way to support Robin at the final ambush site.

There were now just twenty or so cavalry left to deal with, including Guy of Gisborne himself. The chances of a successful mission were now strongly favoured, thanks to Matt, James and the small band of men who accompanied them.

Matt and James decided to ride ahead and quickly left the trail, heading into the forest to thwart the enemy in front of them. Several more riding horses followed, while those on foot made their way more slowly.

"One final ambush to go!" James called to Matt, as they rode off at a swift canter.

"There's going to be some feasting and celebration tonight, that's for sure," Matt replied, already thinking about the venison he planned to consume.

Chapter 14

# Where is Robin?

The boys reached Robin's ambush site quickly and without incident, thanks to the horses they rode. Those travelling behind them on foot would take some time yet, but with every passing minute, the number at the final ambush site swelled.

Matt and James made their way to Robin and relayed the details of what had transpired.

"Ye have done us proud, and probably prevented the bloodshed we were so desperate to avoid with all you have achieved today. There will be many stories told of this adventure in days to come and your names will be known throughout the county," Robin told them, delighted with their contribution and quick thinking. "I was not expecting to seize the treasure before the final showdown and this has helped us achieve our goal, despite anything that might happen now."

By now, Robin's numbers had risen to nearly fifty men, and with only about twenty cavalry remaining, success was looking very promising indeed. Robin organised his men with all the expertise of his soldier's training. He placed archers on the path to block the riders, and sent others to hide in the bushes to follow the last of them, making sure that there was no possible escape. Others he placed in the trees to give them aerial supremacy and finally, the remaining men were positioned along the length of the clearing, hidden in the bushes. To all of these men he gave the single order – to remain concealed until he called out the name of Robin Hood. Then they were to reveal themselves and close in on the enemy.

With everyone in position, Robin stood in the centre of the clearing with Will Scarlet, John Little, Matt and James, calmly awaiting the enemy's arrival. They did not have long to wait before the riders turned the bend in the trail at the other end of the clearing. They were spotted instantly, but as they appeared to be unarmed, the riders continued towards them before a challenge was issued by Guy of Gisborne.

"Who are ye and what are ye doing in the Sheriff's forest?"

"I am waiting," Robin said, calmly.

"Waiting? What are ye waiting for?" asked Gisborne, his patience already running out and not liking the casual manner in which Robin had spoken to him.

"Actually, I was waiting for thee," replied Robin, in the same calm voice.

"What dost thou mean, waiting for me?" asked Gisborne, anger and confusion evident in his voice. "Nobody knows that I am here on this trail right now!"

"Thou art Guy of Gisborne, art thou not? And thy mission is to bring a consignment of treasure to thy cousin the Sheriff of Nottingham, is it not?" Robin asked him.

Guy looked visibly shocked.

"Who art thou?" he shouted. "What is this nonsense of

which thou speaketh?"

"Me? I am Robin Hood," Robin told him, with a smile broadening across his face. "And thou, Sir, art trapped!"

Guy was about to shout something, when men began to appear from their hiding places, surrounding the soldiers, with bows and arrows pointing at them. Noises from above induced him to look up, and he saw even more armed men sitting on branches, pointing their weapons at him.

"Thou hast made a bad mistake, Hood, for I have a large army behind me who, even now, is making its way towards us. Canst thou not hear them?" he almost laughed.

"I cannot say I hear single sound, to tell thee the truth. Mayhap *thou* shouldst indeed look behind and see who is there, for thine army has already been disposed of. There is nothing to see but more of my men!"

Gisborne looked around in vain, indeed seeing only more of Robin's men, and realised that he was trapped.

The vast frame of John Little stood alongside Robin and indicated for the riders to dismount. This they did without resistance. They were disarmed and tied up one by one, until Gisborne was left standing alone.

"I will see thee hang for this, Hood," he shouted, defiantly.

Men moved in and secured him tightly, one peering at him closely.

"I cannot allow thee to talk to Robin like that, 'tis most impolite." And without further delay, he stuffed a piece of cloth into Gisborne's mouth.

Robin gave orders to his men to lead the prisoners through the forest back where they came from, picking up the other captives en route, and forcing them out of

Sherwood Forest. He told them to lead them for three miles beyond the forest and then set them loose, but under no circumstances were they to untie them. Instead, on leaving the forest, they were to cut the clothes from them, leaving them to march in just their undergarments.

He then asked John, Will, Matt and James to head back to their village with the womenfolk and prepare for a great feast, while he selected two riders to accompany him to hunt for more meat to ensure that there was plenty for everyone that evening.

"I have a sudden fancy for some boar!" he declared.

With that, it was all over!

Matt and James headed back to collect the women, and Robin and the two archers disappeared into the forest to hunt.

It was already getting dark by the time most of the Hood's community made it back to the safety of their sanctuary in the centre of Sherwood Forest.

When Matt and James returned, they were greeted by the sounds of happy voices and the smell of meat being roasted over open fires.

Both went to the stream to wash, laughing at as they caught sight of their strange reflections in the still water of the pool again.

The treasure wagon had been left alongside the treasure-trove shelter, and the boys were surprised that it had not yet been uncovered to reveal the rewards of all their endeavours. Matt suggested that it was a task for Robin himself and James had to agree that this was probably what would happen.

Marion was busy with the women, helping to cook

huge roasts. She had stayed behind today under Robin's orders, to help look after the children. Robin had decided that he could not risk her being seen, as she would have been easily recognised and her life would have been put in danger long after the events of the day.

People went to their favourite places in the gathering area and started to eat the food prepared by the women. Matt and James sat with Little John, joined by Will Scarlett at John's invitation. They were discussing the different events that had taken place that day, in between huge mouthfuls of prime venison that almost melted in the mouth.

After a few minutes, Marion came over, asking to speak to John in private. Matt and James took little interest in this, being content to continue eating after the day's efforts, but Will looked concerned as they disappeared into one of the dwellings, deep in discussion. When they reappeared they headed to Robin's place by the old fallen tree and John raised his hands for silence.

The noise died out in an instant. This was unheard of – nobody else ever used Robin's place! It was a courtesy that everyone adhered to, not even Robin's right-hand man had sat there before. It was at that moment that people suddenly became aware that something was wrong.

A baby started to cry, shattering the silence that had descended on the gathering.

"People of the Hood," John started, "despite the success of our mission today, where not a drop of blood was spilt, I fear I bear bad tidings.

"Our beloved leader, Robert, has not yet returned. As many of ye know, he left to hunt boar earlier today for our great celebration tonight. The two men who accompanied him have also failed to return, and this leads me to believe that some mischief has befallen them. Either they have been hurt in a hunting accident or they have been caught by one of the Sheriff's hunting parties. I can think of no other reason that would prevent him from returning to share in our celebration tonight.

"There is but little we can do right now..." his voice faltered with the strength of his emotion, but he suddenly stood up taller as if collecting himself. "At first light, I will take a small group of men to track Robin's journey from the ambush site. In the event that he has been captured, we will send a man into Nottingham to find Friar Tuck, whose knowledge of the happenings there is equal to none other. I know that this is a sorrowful worry for us all, but Robert would want the celebration to continue. What we did today was nothing short of a miracle! We now have enough treasure to pay off the ransom for King Richard. I insist that everybody eats and drinks their fill. Tomorrow we shall begin the search for Robert," he finished, sadly.

With that, John returned to his group and Marion disappeared into the dwelling that she used when she stayed in the forest.

John sat down heavily between Matt and James.

"I want the two of ye with me tomorrow morning. The resourcefulness and quick thinking ye displayed today may well be needed, for verily we have no notion as to what has happened to Robert. I will take Will Scarlett as well – he is the best tracker I have ever known, and his skills may well reveal the turn of events. If he has been taken by the Sheriff's men, his life will most certainly be in danger. Most of us have prices on our heads if we are delivered alive to the Sheriff, but Robin is such a threat that his bounty is the same, whether he is captured dead or alive."

James had never heard him sound so downcast, so worried. He looked John straight in the eyes and clasped his wrist in his hand.

"You can rely on us, John. There is nothing we wouldn't do in return for the generosity and kindness you've all shown us from the beginning. Whatever you need us to do, it will be done. We will track him down and bring him home where he belongs."

"I am grateful to ye, as I am for what ye did today. We will leave at first light – I suggest ye try to get some sleep; it was a long day today and it could be again on the morrow."

John bade them goodnight and disappeared into his house.


The festivities continued for a while longer before people started to return to their dwellings, but the atmosphere had been dampened and the laughter and merriment replaced by hushed tones and subdued, worried frowns. Matt and James stayed up a while longer, discussing what might happen tomorrow. They had spent little time with Will Scarlett so far but had heard of his skill as a tracker from stories shared by several people at communal meals, and they both looked forward to seeing him in action. They knew he was a favourite of the Hood, and wondered what he had done to earn that position. Perhaps they would find out tomorrow.

James announced his intention to bed down for the night – the exhaustion of the day suddenly catching up with him. Matt nodded his acquiescence and the two of them unrolled their sleeping mats.

"It looks like any thoughts of going home will have to be put on hold for the moment," said James. "How can you go from such a high to such a low, in such a short space of time?"

"I know what you mean," replied his friend. "I just hope we can get him back safely. Marion looked wretched with worry."

Unlike previous nights here, the sound of life in the camp was strangely quiet, but sleep did not come easily. Despite their fatigue, they lay awake for more than an hour before drifting into a restless and unsettling sleep.

## Chapter 15

# The Search for Robin

As the first rays of light filtered their way through the forest canopy, silhouetting the trunks of age-old trees, the four rose from their disturbed slumber and packed a few items that they might need for the day ahead.

Marion appeared with a small pack of food for their travels, saying a few private words to John who then led the way with a determined look on his face, setting a fast pace. Will strode effortlessly beside him, followed just behind by Matt and James. It had taken more than two hours to reach the ambush trail yesterday, but John was determined to shave an hour off that, knowing that they didn't have to wait for slower members of the community or indeed transport the equipment they had carried the day before. They intercepted the trail east of the final ambush site in just over an hour. Little had been said en route, but worry and concern was etched on the faces of Robin's friends, John and Will.

Matt and James, who, as yet, did not have the strength of bond with Robin as the other two, had respected their silence, remaining quiet themselves. It took another twenty minutes of walking before they reached the site of yesterday's final ambush when Will broke the silence.

"We shall start at the place where Robin stood and

gave his final instructions before announcing that he was to go hunting. I need to determine which of the many footprints are his in order to track him."

Matt and James instantly looked down to the ground, their faces showed signs of despair as they saw the complete confusion of tangled and broken tracks around them. 'How on earth could anybody read anything from this mess?' they wondered.

Will, however, displayed no such concern and asked John to pick out the spot where Robin had stood, to see if the placement mirrored his own. John walked confidently to the spot he thought was accurate and Will nodded pensively.

"I thought he was slightly forward of that point. Matthew, James – what are your thoughts on this?"

Matt looked quickly towards James and spoke quietly so that the others couldn't hear. "Think of it as a rugby match. Yesterday, we took our positions based on the best line of attack; Robin was behind us but towards the centre of us. I can remember thinking that a large oak tree, to my left, would give me good cover if we needed to retreat under the onslaught of charging horses."

James nodded thoughtfully. "I had a similar thought – only to my right was a thorn bush. I felt sure that the horses would not like to go through that if we had to retreat."

His impatience caused John to interrupt the boys' conversation.

"Well? What do ye think?" he asked, abruptly.

"Give us a moment, John, and I'm sure we can get his position to within a few feet," said Matt, patiently.

"Time is of the essence, lads. Who knows what fate

may have befallen him?" John said, almost angrily.

"We understand that, John. Which is why we need to get it right the first time," said Matt, gently.

Will lay his hand lightly on John's arm to prevent him from saying any more. "Matthew is right. We cannot afford to waste time following the wrong tracks."

Matt moved away from the group and took the same position he had adopted yesterday. He was accurate to within inches. James moved away from him and sought the spot where he himself had stood.

"John! Come and stand between us right in the middle, please," called Matt.

John did as he was asked. Then Matt instructed him to take a few steps backwards until he told him to stop.

"You are exactly where Robin was standing yesterday. There was nobody within a couple of feet of him in any direction, and from there he walked forward to address Guy of Gisborne," James told him, confidently.

Will crouched down at the spot where John stood. "He is right! Thou art exactly behind a set of prints made by a stationary man, facing Gisborne's men." He followed the tracks carefully to a spot where the prints appeared clearly, side by side, and he knew that this was where Robin had delivered his final instructions before leaving to hunt.

Will stood up with a worried look on his face.

"I fear there are good tidings and bad," he told them. "Firstly, Robin's boots are of a more noble quality to ours and are most easy to track. But alas, he hunted on horseback, and as we left the clearing before he did, we have no notion as to the direction he may perchance have taken."

James suddenly had an idea.

"When I went hunting with Robin, he told me that that the northern parts of the forest were the best for hunting boar. I'm sure that, as it was getting late, he would have gone to where he could get a result as quickly as possible."

John nodded his agreement, having heard Robin say that on several different occasions in the past.

"From this place then, he would have walked to a horse," Will told them, assuredly. "Take a look at his tracks and allow me to show ye how they differ from ours."

They all crouched down to look at Robin's footprints.

"See the heel of his boot? Look at the depth of the heel in this soft earth and see the horseshoe shape of it, then compare it to your own which is shallower and more round."

As they stared at it, they could clearly see the difference; now they knew what they were looking for.

Will looked for the next set of Robin's prints, to track where he had walked to, but there were many marks in this area, one on top of another and it took him several minutes before he announced that Robin had moved towards the side of the clearing.

"Forsooth!" exclaimed John, suddenly. "Robin had brought his own horse and left it tethered about twenty paces in that direction." He pointed off towards a small clump of trees at the edge of the clearing. "He always prefers to ride his own horse when hunting. We should seek his trail yonder."

"Aye! Look for areas of soft ground that might show a footprint or two, or seek bits of broken plants that a man's foot may have trampled," ordered Will, setting off in front of the others.

John found a tell-tale heel-print on a damp area of the forest floor, and Will saw evidence of broken twigs and disturbed undergrowth that clearly gave them line and direction into the forest to where Robin had tethered his horse. Within minutes, they found the spot where the horse had been tied and clear imprints of Robin's boots.

"All we have to do now is follow the hoof prints. They will be plain to see on the soft ground and there will be signs of damage where the horses forced through the bushes. By the time we find Robin ye will, in truth, be able to track as well as me," Will told them, delighted with their progress.

A few yards further on, two more sets of hoof-prints joined Robin's. If there had been any doubt that this was Robin's trail before, it was now completely dispelled, and they tracked the three animals for several miles, deep into the forest.

As they walked, they ate some of the bread and cold meat that Marion had prepared for them, reluctant to pause even for a few minutes. Not long afterwards Will found other footprints around the trail they were following.

"These are soldiers' prints," Will told them, concern etched on his face, "but I cannot say if they were made before or after Robin passed this way. There were between six and eight of them."

A little further on, he stopped suddenly at a small clearing.

"They stopped here – look at the ground and ye can see three clear sets of hoof-prints. Why would they stop in the open?"

He searched the ground around them, and soon picked

up the tracks of the three riders who had dismounted there. The tracks led away from the horses for a few yards where they stopped and met with a tangle of other prints, those of the soldiers. Two more sets came towards them from the sides and stopped behind them. Will looked at the others with despair.

"I fear that Robin and the other men have been captured by these soldiers. The evidence here is strong."

"Where would these soldiers have come from and what were they doing so deep in the forest?" James asked, confused.

"'Tis my supposition that this be one of the groups we ambushed yesterday and tied up. Mayhap they escaped and were trying to make their way back when they heard Robin approaching and set a trap for him. The fact that they are so far from the trail suggests they were, perchance, lost and that this was good fortune for them," continued Will, with bitterness in his voice.

"What do we do now then?" asked Matt.

"We follow the trail to see whither they took him, and devise a rescue plan," said John, emphatically.

For the next two hours, they followed the clearly visible trail. They could tell that Robin was now on foot as his heel prints were easily seen in the softer areas, and the horses were not being ridden as their tracks were shallower without the weight of a rider. The route they followed seemed to be directionless and, more than once, they passed the same way that the lost soldiers had led their captives.

By chance they seemed to have stumbled onto a game path and had followed that for some distance before it intersected the ambush trail. Here the path was so disturbed from the previous day's march that tracking once again became difficult. But it was clear that they were heading towards Nottingham castle and right into the Sheriff's lair.

After losing the trail yet again in the failing light, John eventually called a halt to further tracking. It was getting late and they knew beyond any reasonable doubt where Robin had been taken, and it wasn't far before the trail left the safety of Sherwood Forest.

"We have done all we can, for now," said John with a sigh. "'Tis time we returned to advise the others what we know and to start planning how we can rescue Robin before the Sheriff slays him."

They started homewards as they had come, in silence, deep in thought. It was already dark when they finally reached the sanctuary of the forest settlement and the greetings of a hundred concerned members of their community.

John, feeling overwhelmed and harassed by the volume of questions fired at him, ordered the people to gather at the meeting place shortly, while he and his travelling companions rested and ate.

Exactly one hour later, John stood in Robin's place and told the community everything they had discovered that day. The initial optimism that people had shown upon their return was immediately replaced with concern and anguish. Many of the women cried openly while the men were unusually subdued.

Although John did his best to instil confidence and assure them that plans were afoot to rescue Robin and his companions, he could not fully disguise the concern in his voice and the worry etched upon his face. After his brief talk concluded, with heavy hearts and troubled minds, they silently made their way to their beds, each person lost in thought at what Robin might be enduring at that very moment at the hands of the Sheriff's men. Such nightmarish contemplation made sleep impossible for the majority of folk during that long, difficult night.

## Chapter 16

# A Plan is Hatched

The next morning John gathered the leaders of the community together in the building that Robin used for such meetings.

"Two of us shall venture to the castle to determine exactly where Robin is held. They can garb themselves as farm labourers and take a small cart of produce to sell. This will allow them to move freely within the castle walls and seek the information we need. Mayhap Mary Tailor can be persuaded to draw a likeness of the castle and its grounds to help us plan Robin's escape," he told them.

Will explained that Mary was known for her drawing skills and could even reproduce a very good likeness of a face from a verbal description, if needed. All members of the community had been within the castle walls at some time in the past, and some had even been in the castle itself. Mary's husband was a tailor of some standing and had designed and made clothes for many of the nobility who lived in the castle. As such, he had been able to move around the castle with relative ease and would have first-hand knowledge of its layout.

Mary, as a lady of note, also knew the castle well. John sent one of the leaders to find her, and she and her husband appeared within a few minutes. John explained what he needed and she soon set to work, drawing the castle and grounds on the surface of a large table as there was no parchment at the campsite. It was decided to wait until she had finished before making plans, so John disbanded the meeting and set about organising a husband-and-wife team to travel to Nottingham and enter the castle grounds.

Just before noon, Marion appeared at John's dwelling with Mary at her side.

"Mistress Mary has completed her task, John. The castle is so clearly drawn that I vouchsafe a child could find their way just by looking at it."

John thanked Mary and asked that she and her husband remain. Then he asked Will to assemble the leaders at the meeting house once more.

Before he had finished speaking, however, a shout ahead warned him of an imminent arrival at the campsite, and he looked up towards the path leading down from the ridge. There, on a horse-drawn cart, sat Friar Tuck who appeared to be in some hurry to descend the slope. The cart swayed and juddered as its wooden wheels encountered roots and rocks, the harness buckles clanking as the monk fought with the reins.

"Methinks the goodly Friar has tidings to share," said Will, watching the hasty descent of the monk.

"Go, do as I have instructed, Will, and I shall bring the Friar forthwith. He can share his news with all at the meeting house and save us precious time," John told him with a surfeit of feelings welling up inside him.

Even as the Friar started to dismount from the cart with his back to his intended audience, John could hear the rumble of his deep voice as he tried to share the latest news.

"Save it till we reach the meeting house," ordered John and led him along the path.

Matt and James followed them in quickly, immediately struck by the image of the castle grounds that had been depicted on the large table within the room. The paths and various buildings were clearly shown and the castle itself appeared in cross-section with each room carefully labelled, and in such detail, that they stared awestruck at Mary's achievements. The Friar marvelled openly at the intricacies the picture portrayed.

"Ye know then what has taken place?" he asked the assembled company.

"That Robin was taken to the castle, aye, but alas no more than that," said Will.

"Allow me to fill in some of the details for ye then," said Tuck, relishing being the centre of attention. "Tell me what ye know and I will continue henceforth."

Will relayed events as he understood them from the tracks. Tuck nodded in agreement but said nothing until Will got to the part where Robin arrived at the castle.

"Thine interpretation of the tracks is most accurate, Will Scarlet, and I commend thee as a master tracker," he started.

Will glowed at the compliment.

"At the castle, Robin was placed in the tower for questioning. When it became clear that he could not easily be induced to break his silence, he was beaten. Then he was moved to the dungeons for the Sheriff's instruments of torture to be used. In truth, he was near to death at one point, and the Sheriff had to halt proceedings to allow the wretched man time to recover his senses. He has stated his intention to hang Robin at the castle gallows this Saturday coming and is planning a feast to celebrate the impending death of 'Nottingham's most feared villain'. In the meantime, the Sheriff has returned Robin to the tower with the attentions of his personal physician to ensure he is well enough to walk to his own hanging," Tuck informed them.

There was a loud sob and Marion half-fell onto one of the benches with her hands clasped to her mouth.

"Oh Robin!" she cried. "We have to get him back. They cannot kill him!"

Mary sat down beside her and gathered her close. "I know 'tis hard," she said, fervently, "but thou must be brave, dearheart. Robin Hood will return to us, I know it!"

Even Friar Tuck could not prevent the moistening of his eyes at the strength of the women's reactions. He felt the loss of his friend as much as any of the Hood's people.

"We have but three days to plan and effect Robin's rescue then," said Will, wretchedly.

John nodded slowly, then looked round at the others with a glimmer of hope shining in his eyes. "Aye, but if the Sheriff has organised a feast, it will surely mean that the castle will be full of people and distractions, which can only help our cause."

The group agreed and soon the talking and planning became more positive and the size of the task less daunting. Slowly, as ideas were discussed and a possible plan emerged, their fear of failure and their repugnance at the very idea of life without Robin Hood began to retreat into the background, assuming more manageable proportions again. Even Marion regained her strength and determination, joining in the planning with the leaders in her usual forthright manner, her earlier hopelessness forgotten.

After more than two hours of discussion, it became clear that rescue from the tower would be almost impossible and, therefore, the only realistic opportunity to rescue him would be as he was marched to the gallows.

Friar Tuck and Marion stayed in the meeting house, marking the oversized map with the positions of the sentries and other foot soldiers, both inside the castle and outside in the grounds, while the others went outside for a break and some food.

They had just finished their meal, when Marion and Tuck appeared with bowls of venison stew and sat down beside them to eat. What Marion said next put their thoughts into a whirlwind of doubt and worry.

"The goodly Friar and myself estimate there to be between 150 and 200 soldiers within the castle grounds. Of course, not all will be on duty; the night guards will be resting in the barrack rooms, but even if every one of us here enters the castle grounds, we shall still be outnumbered nearly two to one," she said, forlornly.

Matt spoke up quickly, sensing the mood becoming increasingly negative. "We can reduce those odds significantly if we took some of them out of action," he said.

"How so?" asked John.

"For a start, if we locked in those who are resting in the barracks, they will be of no further concern to us," Matt replied.

John asked Marion for an estimate of the number who might be in there.

"As few as fifty and no more than seventy," she said, making a mental calculation of the number of guards stationed inside the castle and on the battlements.

"The numbers are still against us, but they are better," said John with a glimmer of hope. "If we could but tie up another hundred, verily we could have a fighting chance!"

James made the next suggestion.

"Perhaps we are looking at this from the wrong angle. Maybe it's not how many we tie up but more about removing the ones who offer the most danger to us."

"Verily, I like thy way of thinking, James, and I understand the point thou makest, but we shall still need to take out a great number to increase our chance of escape after we rescue Robin," interjected Will.

One of the other leaders spoke up.

"Mayhap we are thinking the wrong way completely. At the moment, we are trying to achieve what is nigh on impossible, but there is one thing I know about the Sheriff of Nottingham, 'tis that his greed is bigger than any other man's – forsooth, 'tis most legendary! Mayhap we should offer to trade Robin for the treasure. Verily, he could not resist that. If we were to make the trade in the forest on our own ground, we could perchance achieve our target."

"'Tis a goodly notion, Mark, but Robin would not risk losing the treasure we have secured for the release of King Richard. He would happily die for him," said John, forlornly.

"Then we must barter with something else, but what thing shall it be?" continued Mark.

"What about the Sheriff himself?" James suggested, excitedly. "What if we were to kidnap the Sheriff instead of rescuing Robin, then force an exchange of the two of them? If we could get him to Sherwood Forest before they attack us, we would have the best bargaining tool we could want."

"In the time it takes us to walk from the castle to the forest edge, these soldiers with their horses would surround us, and cut us down like cornstalks," said John.

"So we need a delaying tactic – one that will give us time to cross the open ground. If we cut the drawbridge ropes on departure, it would take them some time to make the repairs."

John nodded thoughtfully at the idea. "But by what means are we to kidnap the Sheriff? He will be most securely guarded."

"The Sheriff will not be as well guarded as we might think," said Matt. "For one thing, he might be expecting a rescue attempt to be made and, as such, I think his men's attention will be firmly placed on Robin. Secondly, he will be wallowing in self-importance at his successful arrest of Robin, which no doubt he will take sole credit for. I think he will be singing his own praises to as many people as he can!"

"Thy words might just hold truth! If we create a wave of pressure from the back of the crowd gathered to witness the hanging, some of us may be able to seize him. The guards would not fire upon the crowd with him in its midst. They may not like him, but they are loyal to him and are paid a goodly sum to keep that loyalty. I sense the beginning of a good scheme here.

"Let us return to the meeting-house and contrive a plan to these ends," said John, with a fresh gleam of determination.

One of the biggest problems was how to evade the

Sheriff's men after the exchange had taken place, and it was James who came up with the idea of using the covered traps along the ambush trail again. They could use the traps to hide in and the final exchange could be made with as few as three or four men visible. The only ones at risk would be those few. The others would appear to have vanished. A few well-placed women to start wailing and moaning the haunting chants they had used before might well dissuade the soldiers from even searching for them. After all, Sherwood was haunted, wasn't it? The last few men would have horses waiting for them and ride off into the depths of the forest, drawing the soldiers away from where the Hood's men were hidden. It was starting to look like a simple but genius plan, but they all knew that it would take careful preparation, split-second timing, as well as an element of luck if it was going to succeed.

The plans were finalised over the following few hours and it was decided that several teams would be sent to the ambush trail to make improvements to the traps and to dig others to hide the men of Sherwood. All this would take time though, and they had precious little of that to work with.

Chapter 17

# Judgement Day

Over the next couple of days, James spent all his time on the trail supervising a team that widened the holes and enlarged the trap covers. The work was tiring and seemingly endless.

John had organised his people into small groups to infiltrate Nottingham Castle under a variety of disguises. He did not want to leave anything to chance. Once in, they were to stay there until the morning of the execution, when they would take up their positions. Another reason for this early deployment was so that no unusually large groups of people turned up to arouse suspicion, or perhaps even be turned away. Of course, there was a risk that some of the people might be recognised, but it was a risk they were all willing to take. John, Will, and the other leaders would enter at different times the day before, as they were more widely known and this would, hopefully, reduce the risk of being caught.

Matt and James would arrive on the final morning and they had been given a task that would either make or break the whole plan. It was down to them to take control of the castle gate supported by two others already in the castle grounds. Although honoured to be given such an important mission, both boys could not help but feel the weight of responsibility as well. After all, Robin's life and the escape of many depended on a successful outcome. Failure was unthinkable...

And so came the morning of the execution.

Matt and James were travelling with a cart of some of Friar Tuck's strongest ale, with the intention of sharing more than a healthy dose of it with some of the soldiers whose duties they were about to relieve. As they crossed the drawbridge into the castle, they were stopped and the wagon searched before they were allowed to enter.

The number of people present was huge; masses of them moved about the castle grounds with no small degree of difficulty. The boys pulled up their cart at the rear of the crowd, as near to the gate guards as they could without raising suspicion. Then, under full sight of the guards, they appeared to drink heavily and were soon playing the role of partly-intoxicated men. They were joined by their two comrades who would help secure the gates, and who also joined in the heavy-drinking charade.

Matt could see some of the Hood's men to the rear, keeping out of the crowd of people. When the time was right, it would be they who would instigate the crush. From his vantage point standing on the cart, he could make out a line of the Hood's men that stretched through the depth of the crowd right up to the front of the gallows. The castle door from which the Sheriff would make his appearance was guarded, and a clear path leading to the gallows was roped off to allow him free movement. Matt could just make out John and Will standing directly in front of the gallows and knew that they were the two who intended to grab the Sheriff. His attention was drawn to James who began to sing very loudly and lurch about, as if completely drunk. One of the guards came across and struck him a blow across the side of the head, sending him reeling to the floor. He stayed there unmoving.

Matt poured some ale into a tankard and offered it to the soldier.

"Thou must be hot in all that armour on a day like this. Here, have a drink on me, and send over thy comrades to take one too. 'Tis not every day we get to see a hanging, especially one of this importance!" he said, using the old world language to stay in character and maintain his disguise.

"I shall be glad when 'tis all finished, I tell thee that. Thou art right – 'tis hot and made even hotter by this great throng of people. I thank thee kindly, thy generosity is most welcome." He took the tankard and returned to his post.

Three other soldiers came to collect their drinks, while James made a big scene of getting up and falling straight back down again before managing to get back to the wagon. Many more drinks were given to the guards during the next hour or so.

An hour before noon, the Sheriff made his appearance along with his cousin, Guy of Gisborne. They ambled round the crowd enjoying the attention and cheers of the people, as they threw a few coins, watching in amusement as people scrambled and fought to retrieve them from the dusty ground.

"See how generous your Sheriff is!" he shouted, signalling to the guards at the door from which he had emerged.

The guard opened the door and a procession of cooks brought out freshly roasted venison and sweet-smelling loaves of bread.

"Eat your fill and be ready for the main attraction of this gathering, for today ye will see the demise of the so-called Robin Hood. No more will he steal from the people of this land, and his reign of terror in Sherwood Forest will be over for ever!" he shouted, continuing to scatter handfuls of coins around.

John had seen Gisborne's appearance with the Sheriff and had immediately turned his back. Although he was heavily disguised, there were few men as immense as he was, so he decided to sit down to avoid being noticed. Many of his men followed suit and, before long, others in the crowd joined them, creating a picnic-type scenario that allowed him to blend completely into insignificance.

Gisborne left the Sheriff's side at just five minutes to noon, heading for the castle entrance, while the Sheriff made his way to the front of the crowd opposite John Little. He raised his hands for silence and slowly the din from the crowd subsided until there was barely a whisper to be heard.

"My people! Many of ye know and understand how I have suffered during the reign of Robin Hood and the tyranny he has imposed on my lands. Many of ye have suffered an increase in taxes after the riches of our great county have been stolen by this man. I tell ye – this ends now, for today ye shall behold the punishment of the most reprehensible brigand that Nottingham has ever seen. Ye shall witness the hanging of Robin Hood!

"The stolen treasure is yet to be recovered, but once Hood has been sent to the devil, a systematic search of Sherwood Forest will commence until all that he has stolen has been found and returned to its rightful place.

"So, as the hour approaches noon, let us see how great this 'people's hero' truly is. Let every man, woman and child here today know that Robin Hood is no 'friend of the people'. He is, in fact, nothing more than a common thief!"

He paused, as if waiting for his announcement to be cheered, but it was met with a stony silence from the crowd. The Sheriff was visibly displeased by this and turned away from the crowd to stay his anger. Once composed, he signalled to Guy of Gisborne who was standing by the castle door. Guy took his sword and theatrically rapped on the door three times, to which the door swung open.

Flanked by several guards, Robin emerged. One or two of the crowd stood up to get a better view, followed by others as their views were blocked, until everyone was standing.

This was not the Robin Hood his people were used to seeing. This was a man who had clearly suffered brutal torture over the past few days. His clothes were tattered, and his body covered in blood from the horrors that had been inflicted upon him. His head hung low, almost as if it were too heavy for his neck to support, and he limped badly, scarcely able to lift and place one leg in front of the other.

Guy prodded him in the back with his sword to keep him moving towards the gallows where the noose awaited him, but the Sheriff hadn't finished with him yet and intercepted them before they were halfway to the scaffold.

"See here, people! Before ye, the legendary Robin

Hood – the indestructible Robin Hood, the uncatchable Robin Hood! See how he bleeds! Does this look like a person that deserves such epithets? Nay, I say. He is but a man and a thief – a common thief. He has tried the patience of your Sheriff for too long and, verily, t'was my own daring and cunning that caught him in the oft-called 'haunted' Sherwood Forest – the place where Hood lived, hiding like a fox in a hole. Now we shall see if he dies like a man or begs for mercy and my forgiveness for the crimes he has committed."

The Sheriff signalled Guy to recommence Robin's delivery to the gallows while he, once more, returned to his position close to Little John.


It was at that moment that John made his move.

"My lord Sheriff!" he called out in a clear voice. "Thou canst not hang Robin Hood."

The Sheriff stepped towards John, standing right in front of him. He drew his sword and pointed it at John's chest.

"Who are thee to question my authority?" he asked in disbelief at the challenge this man had made.

"I, my lord, am John Little, friend of Robin Hood, and if thou hangst him, it shall be the last thing on earth that thou shalt ever do," John stated, calmly.

Before the Sheriff had time to digest what had been said, John knocked his sword to the side. The momentum forced the Sheriff to turn slightly to maintain his balance, and as he did so, John grabbed him around the neck in a vice-like grip, relieving him of his sword in the same movement. He took the Sheriff's own knife from its sheath, holding it to his throat.

"Believe me when I say that if Robin continues towards those steps, I shall slit thy throat from ear to ear," John growled into his ear.

The effect of the threat was instantaneous and the Sheriff's body began to shake uncontrollably. Guy, too, began to regain his composure after the initial shock at what had just happened, and called for the guards who emerged, as if from nowhere, to stand in front of the Sheriff and the crowd.

"Tell thy men to move away this instant, or I shall carry out my threat," continued Little John. The Sheriff complied and the soldiers took several paces backwards.

"Gisborne!" called John. "Thou and I are going to make a trade; a life for a life. I want Robin Hood and thou wantst thy cousin."

"That sounds like a fair trade, let us commence! Send the Sheriff to me and I shall send thee Robin Hood," suggested Gisborne.

"The trade is not to happen here, Gisborne. It shall take place in Sherwood Forest at a time and place of my choosing," replied John, confidently.

"Look around thee, Little! Dost thou really think I shall let thee leave the castle?"

"Thou hast but little choice in the matter – it shall be as I say. Shall it not, Sheriff?" said John, increasing the pressure on the Sheriff's neck.

"Aye, aye! Do as he says, cousin!" choked the Sheriff.

Gisborne spat at the ground, showing his contempt for his cousin's cowardice.

"We shall leave now and thou willst bring Robin to the trading area," said John, still utterly calm but letting Gisborne know that he was in complete charge of the situation.

John began moving backwards, the crowd opening up on either side of him, allowing him unimpeded freedom of movement. The look of terror in the Sheriff's eyes kept Gisborne at bay. He followed them just a few yards away, not once releasing eye contact with John, a growing number of soldiers behind him.

Passing his men on either side, John could see them making their way through the crowd towards the castle gate, and in that moment, any doubts he might have felt at pulling this off were dispelled from his mind. As he approached the rear of the crowd, he eyed his fellow leaders who, at John's almost imperceptible nod, called out to the rest of their people, "Now!"

At the signal, Robin Hood's men pushed with all their might at the hordes in front of them, triggering an immediate domino effect. Many of the crowd fell to the ground, while others collided with the people in front of them. The disarray spilled into the soldiers following Gisborne, as they too were sent lurching into those around them. It was complete chaos and exactly what the plan had called for.

Chapter 18

# The Trade

Matt and James had watched the events unfolding in front of them and, with their two collaborators, had easily overpowered the four semi-drunk guards – the gate was now under their control. Matt had studied the mechanisms for lifting the portcullis and was pleased that ropes were used rather than chains. This meant that the portcullis could easily be brought down by cutting through the ropes attached to the pulleys, and the time needed to replace them would allow for a safe return to Sherwood.

James had suggested they use the ale wagon to transport John and the Sheriff back to the forest; with the Sheriff standing in open view of the castle, the guards would be unlikely to let loose their arrows on them.

The Hood's men began streaming through the gate, with John, the Sheriff and the four temporary gatekeepers the last to exit. John dragged the terrified Sheriff through the archway surrounding the gate while Matt and James began hacking at the portcullis' ropes with their swords. They were thick and covered in grease, and it took several blows before they were even halfway through. Matt ordered his two colleagues to go with John, and when the rope strands still supporting the iron portcullis started to snap under the tension, he and James took their place alongside the others. They were just clear of the portcullis when the ropes finally gave way with a loud crack and the heavy gate came crashing down. They all clambered aboard the cart behind the Sheriff.

John called out to Gisborne, peering through the iron crosspieces of the grating, as they started to pull away.

"The exchange shall take place one hour hence on the trail through the forest, Gisborne. Try not to be behind time! And in the name of the Almighty, put Robin on a horse. If he suffers any more, it shall be nothing compared to the pain I shall inflict on your cousin," he said, pressing harder with the knife he still held to the Sheriff's throat, hoping to elicit a reaction from him. He was not disappointed.

"Do as he says, Guy!" pleaded the Sheriff. "I beg thee – just do as he says!"

The ground they had to cover would normally take a good ten minutes, but the band of men did it in five, and as Matt looked back, he could just make out the portcullis being heaved open with the help of stout wooden staves. James saw it too and said, to nobody in particular, "So far, so good!"

They knew the Sheriff's forces would catch up with them soon; they could not hope to outrun any force on horseback, and as they travelled along the ambush trail, it was not long before the noise caused by the hundred or so cavalry that pursued them sent vibrations through the forest floor beneath their feet. James estimated it would take just a few more minutes before they reached the first of their concealed hiding places, but they would probably be caught up with before they reached it.

John stood calmly on the wagon at the rear of the group of men, still with the Sheriff locked in his vice-like grip, waiting for the first glimpse of the fast-approaching horsemen. He didn't have to wait long until the first came into sight.

Sir Guy Gisborne travelled fourth in line, not wanting to expose himself directly to possible attack. The riders eased to a slow walk about twenty yards from John's position.

"Let us make the exchange, John Little!" he called out.

"In a few short moments, Gisborne," John replied, calmly. "Where is Robin Hood? Bring him to the front so that I may see there has been no foul play," he demanded.

Gisborne spoke to one of the men riding alongside him, who turned his horse back the way he had come and disappeared from view.

While they waited, the Hood's men reached the first of the concealed hideaways and the six of them disappeared beneath the disguised thatched coverings, completely out of sight of the enemy. Two more groups of men disappeared from the trail in the same way, before Robin Hood, mounted on a horse, was led to the front of the enemy's line.

It was clear that Robin was in a bad way, his head sagging forwards, chin on chest, and his body swaying awkwardly from side to side with the horse's movement.

"Here he is, Little. This is what thou wantst – why do we not stop here and make the trade?" Gisborne enquired, with a malicious edge to his voice.

"There is a clearing a short way up the trail. We shall make the exchange there – where I can see all of thy men and ensure thou dost not deviate from the agreement we made," John told him in the same calm voice that was beginning to annoy Gisborne.

In fact, John had decided to do the exchange at the narrowest part of the path and was just biding his time until all of his men had concealed themselves. As they rounded the next bend in the trail, the last of the men on foot were safely hidden away, with the remaining few on the cart. In total, just five of them, along with the Sheriff, were left.

Matt and James picked up their bows and loaded arrows as discreetly as they could, while the cart came to a stop. Their two colleagues also picked up their weapons and moved from their position behind John into the open, where they could be seen by Gisborne. John released his grip on the Sheriff, telling him to remain completely still. The Sheriff, seeing that they all had their arrows pointed directly at him, was too afraid to disobey.

"I have changed my mind, Gisborne. We shall do the trade here," John called out.

"So be it," replied Gisborne. "How dost thou want to proceed?"

As John began to give instructions, there was a movement behind him, out of sight of Gisborne and his soldiers. Horses had been left tethered to the trees for their escape and one of John's men was quietly untying them, before slinking back to his concealed lair. John could see that Robin was in no shape to ride in difficult terrain through the forest and had changed his original plan. He sent the Sheriff forward three paces and ordered him to stop while he announced his intentions to Matt and James. They grinned at his proposal and eagerly took on the responsibility of the task he required of them. They, in turn, told their two companions who immediately disappeared from view, moving down the trail to the next hiding place and lowering the cover above them.

Gisborne ordered one of his men to help Robin from his horse, then instructed the poor, injured man to take the same three paces forward that the Sheriff had made.

Matt lowered his bow, disappearing behind the cart and came forward leading two horses. He mounted one and reloaded his bow. James followed his example, but instead of pointing his arrow at the Sheriff, he pointed it straight at Gisborne.

"What deception is this?" demanded Gisborne, angrily.

"There is no deception here, Gisborne," replied James. "Just a little 'insurance' in case you have a sudden change of heart. If any of your men move off the trail or raise a weapon towards any of us... Well, I don't need to say any more. Let's see if we can complete this trade without bloodshed."

He ordered the Sheriff to take three more paces and Gisborne responded with a similar order to Robin. Another three were taken until Robin and the Sheriff were standing alongside each other.

Robin raised his head slightly so he could look upon this man who had so completely exploited the people under his charge. The Sheriff was taken aback by the cold, clear gaze Robin imposed on him, and looked away. They continued to move away from each other until they were almost safe, when John called for the Sheriff to stand still once more. James and Matt's bows had not wavered from their respective targets when John whispered, "Now!"

Robin's seemingly beaten figure moved forward at lightning speed. He, along with John Little, disappeared behind the wagon and down the trail to where Will stood waiting, holding up another cover. As the two men fell into the hole, Will followed, pulling down the cover.

"You have broken the agreements of our trade," Gisborne shouted, angrily.

One of his soldiers started to raise his crossbow towards James, but James immediately let his arrow fly. It hit the soldier's shield inches above his raised hand, exactly where he had intended. The man dropped his crossbow in shock, while James calmly loaded another arrow with the swift, easy manner of an experienced bowman.

The Sheriff cried out in fear, ordering his men not to take up their arms.

"If you are ready, Gisborne, we can finish the trade," said Matt and ordered the Sheriff to move forward once more. As he took his first cautious step, Matt and James wheeled their horses around and sped off down the ambush trail. There was a few seconds' delay before their swift movements registered with Gisborne, and yet more time elapsed as they were forced to negotiate the heavy cart before giving chase along the narrow trail.

Matt and James rode flat out for a mile before turning off the trail and travelling deeper into Sherwood Forest. Gisborne and the Sheriff gave chase, but it was some time before their anger had dissipated enough for them to realise that all the Hood's men had vanished and they were pursuing only the two on horseback.

As they reached the point where Matt and James had left the trail, they stopped and, deploying their men in groups of ten, sent them forwards at angles to their present position, thus covering more ground in their search. The deeper they ventured into the forest, the less light that reached the ground, blocked by the thick canopy of the trees.

Matt and James were used to the dim light in the dense forest and rode on confidently, using what they could occasionally see of the sun to give them a rough direction. They were several miles east of the Hood's camp and heading south, well away from it. Their plan was to keep going until it became dark, when it would be safe enough to return to the community. It would not be long before the Sheriff's men would give up their pursuit, either through tiredness or fear, as eerie cries and sounds continued to permeate the forest.

After another hour of travelling, they slowed the pace further and dismounted, allowing the horses to rest while they walked. They had heard nothing in the way of cavalry chasing them for some time, and were content in the knowledge that they were safe.

By the time the light started to fade, the boys changed direction and headed directly to Robin's camp, knowing it would be completely dark before they reached it.

While James and Matt led the army away from the hidden men, Will had risen from the security of his hole and travelled back down the trail to the next one. He instructed the men hidden there to start heading back to the campsite and sent one of them to the next hole to pass on the news.

Two hours later, nearly all of the men had returned to the camp as well as some of the women who had left the castle shortly after the soldiers. Marion was there to greet each person as they returned, giving her personal thanks for their part in rescuing Robin.

Robin himself took a little longer getting back, still suffering from the effects of the past few days. As he was assisted down the incline to the camp, everybody was waiting for him and formed a guard of honour to welcome him home. He shook people weakly by the hand before finally collapsing, exhausted, and so was carried into his dwelling by his longstanding friend, John.

Chapter 19

# Decisions

"I think we should let the horses go," said James, suddenly. "While I feel pretty certain that we are no longer being followed, it's clear that the horses are leaving a trail, especially when we pass over softer ground. We don't want to risk the security of the campsite, however slight the risk. We can easily walk the rest of the way."

"You're right," Matt replied, thoughtfully. "Let's release them now. It's starting to get dark, and the going will be easier if we don't have to keep deviating from a direct course."

James stopped walking and turned to the horses following dutifully behind them. He rubbed each gently on their nose speaking softly to them before turning them round. Then, with a swift slap on their rumps, he set them off in the direction they had come from. They were out of sight in seconds. An hour later, the boys were just considering the possibility that they might, in fact, be lost, when they saw a soft glow between the trees, some way ahead.

"Looks like we aren't lost, after all," said Matt, not bothering to hide the relief he felt at the prospect of hot food and a good night's sleep.

As they approached the top of the ridge above the community, they were challenged by an unseen voice.

"Who goes there?"

Clearly, the guards were still out in force, defending the safety of the camp's residents.

"Matthew Smith and James Thatcher!" replied Matt.

There came a loud thump as a figure, hidden in the tree above, dropped to the forest floor revealing a grinning Will Scarlet, looking very pleased to see them.

"We were beginning to think, perchance, ye had been caught."

Matt grinned back at him. "Let's just say that we have explored all of the more scenic parts of Sherwood Forest in our efforts to ensure we weren't being followed! Is everybody back safe and sound?"

"There are a few women not yet returned. They will return in the next few days but, for now, are staying on in Nottingham, keeping their ears open for any possible reprisals the Sheriff might be planning," Will told them.

"What about Robin? He looked in a really bad way the last time we saw him."

"He was badly tortured but will heal, given time. In a few days, he will be up and around as sprightly as a chicken in the springtime!

"Let us go down to the camp, for ye must be vastly hungry. There are many people who would like to thank ye for your efforts since you came to us."

Will called out to another hidden guard, saying that he would be back to relieve him before long, and then led the boys down the path. As they descended, a few well-wishers called out greetings and news of their arrival quickly spread throughout the settlement. As they reached the bottom, it seemed that the whole camp had turned out to welcome them. Their backs and upper arms were bruised by the many thumps and slaps of friendly greeting, as each man sought to address them personally.

At last they reached the end of the large gathering and only John Little's giant frame stood on the path in front of them. He said nothing, preferring for once to greet each of them with an enormous bear hug.

"Ye are the last!" he said. "We have accomplished such an array of things this past week, and all without the loss of a single person. There is much that the two of ye have done that we may never be able to thank ye for properly, but I tell ye this – ye have earned my respect and gratitude, and will have mine undying friendship for as long as I remain on this earth. And I intend for that to be a very long time!

"Come, ye must have a hunger! Heather shall serve you some food."

He led the way into his home and called for Heather who embraced the boys with the same emotion as her husband. They sat down together, as they had many times before, and were tucking in to venison stew before they knew it.

John allowed them to eat before asking them to relay their adventures in the forest. He was satisfied that they had not been followed and had been traversing the forest for longer than necessary but was grateful for their caution.

After much food and conversation, they were just about to turn in for the night when Marion suddenly appeared before them. They stood to greet her and she surprised them both by embracing each of them in a delicate, lady-like hug.

"I cannot thank ye enough for what ye have done for Robin, the people of the forest, and our King!" she said. "I know ye must be exhausted after all your exertions, but Robin has requested your presence and would be honoured if ye came to his abode, as he is not well enough to seek your company hither."

"Of course we'll come," James told her, graciously. "It would be good to see that he is recuperating after his awful ordeal with the Sheriff."

Marion led the way to the dwelling that Robin used. Very few of the community had ever set foot in there, and Matt and James were surprised to find it as sparsely furnished as the others they had been invited into.

Robin lay in his bed, looking gaunt and weak but managed to greet them with a smile. He clasped each of them by the arm in greeting, before speaking.

"I am so pleased that ye managed to get away, unhurt, after all we have achieved. It would have been a grievous thing if ye had not made it safely back. There is little I can say to thank ye for everything ye have done for us these past weeks, but I want ye to know that your King will reward you handsomely upon his return. Both King and country shall be forever in your debt."

"It took many of the people of Sherwood to achieve all that we have. Each has contributed and put their life on the line – we did no more than them, Robin," said James, beginning to feel a little embarrassed by the tributes he and Matt were receiving.

"That is true, but few have instigated so many ideas and strategies that made all this achievable. Ye are testament to the fact that just because a man is born poor, it does not mean that he has nothing of value to offer a society, especially one like ours. Ye will receive the same plot of land from me as all the other people of Sherwood and maybe something else from our King when he returns."

The boys thanked Robin and left him to rest, but not before being made to promise to return the following day at noon to discuss some other plan that Robin wanted to put in motion.

"The trouble is," said Matt, "we might be heroes here, but who's going to believe us when we get back home? We'll have to make the most of our fifteen minutes of fame while we can!"

"How can we tell anybody what's happened? They'd think we're insane! We've been staying here for weeks, but it won't seem like more than a few hours to anyone at home, by the time we get back."

After a good night's rest they returned to Robin's house to be briefed on the mission to get the treasure abroad to pay off the ransom. Robin asked them first for their thoughts and ideas and then for their companionship on the journey.

Although they took the invitation as an honour, James had been thinking about returning to their own world, and as soon as they left, he took Matt aside and suggested that now might be a good time to go back through the waterfall.

"I've been thinking the same thing; Robin's safe now and so's the treasure. Don't get me wrong, this has been a fantastic adventure, but I've a feeling that Robin's trip abroad is going to take a very long time and I'd feel a bit weird being that much further from home. Besides, I'd quite like to see where the waterfall will lead us next time," said Matt.

"I'm going to miss all the people we've met here," said James, with feeling. "They're such a community, working together for a common goal. I wish we could subtly get a few pictures of them before we go, but my battery's totally dead – I checked last night."

"Don't you think we've coped pretty well without all the gadgets we're used to?"

"I suppose we've had other things on our minds. We've certainly been kept pretty busy since we've been here!"

The boys' discussion continued for some time before they agreed to collect their bags and just quietly slip away from the camp to follow the path back to the waterfall.

The trek back through the forest took longer than they had expected, probably because so much had happened to break up their original journey to the settlement in the forest. They stopped at each of the places that brought back a recent memory – memories that would stay with them forever. The stream where they charged at – and flattened – John Little; the spot where they encountered the first character from this place, William Cooper; and the fallen tree where they had hidden from the fearful unknown creatures that had turned out to be nothing more than wild pigs. As they left the wood they immediately spotted their exit from this strange yet amazing world.

As they approached the waterfall, they paused to look back at the view amongst the trees of Sherwood Forest, and the shafts of light penetrating the canopy, casting a soft glow on the forest floor.

"It's a special place, James," said Matt, looking at the forest affectionately.

"You're right there, but now I want to go to another special place. Home!"

They turned and clambered up the rocks to the ledge leading behind the waterfall and started to edge along it. The water cascaded down in front of them, sealing off their final glimpse of the forest and then, suddenly, they were back in the cave where it had all begun.

"Can you believe it? We went there as kids but came back heroes! Who would have thought it? I wonder if we'll ever be able to go there again?" asked James.

"I doubt it. Every time we went out, we saw a different landscape. I'll tell you what though," replied Matt, already anticipating another adventure, "our next journey starts somewhere out there!"

James looked over at his friend, grinning from ear to ear. *It certainly will,* he thought...

C.S. Clifford has always been passionate about stories and storytelling. As a child he earned pocket money singing at weddings in the church choir; the proceeds of which were spent in the local bookshop.

He has taught in primary schools for the past ten years and was inspired to start writing through the constant requests of the children he teaches. He lives in Kent where, when not writing or teaching, he enjoys carpentry and both sea and freshwater angling.

*Walking with the Hood* is his first book.

www.csclifford.co.uk

# Also by C. S. Clifford

Having discovered the waterfall cavern earlier that summer,
Matt and James couldn't wait to see where the mysterious
portal would take them next.

They didn't have to wait long to find out...

Walking out into the breathtaking landscape of the Scottish
Highlands, they discover that they haven't travelled very far
back in time at all. It's the late 1960s, and in a small village just
outside Inverness, international Nessie hunters have arrived!

All seems fine at first, but appearances can be deceptive.
The boys soon learn that the visitors' sinister plans could put
Nessie's life in danger - as well as their own.